Some Night My Prince Will Come

Michel Tremblay

translated by Sheila Fischman

Talonbooks
2004

Talonbooks
P.O. Box 2076, Vancouver, British Columbia, Canada V6B 3S3
www.talonbooks.com

Typeset in Scala and printed and bound in Canada by AGMV Marquis.
Printed on 100% post-consumer recycled paper.

First Printing: September 2004

First published in French in 1995 as *La Nuit des Princes Charmants* by Les
Editions Leméac, Montreal and Actes Sud, France.

LIBRARY AND ARCHIVES CANADA CATALOGUING IN PUBLICATION

Tremblay, Michel, 1942-
[Nuit des princes charmants. English]
    Some night my prince will come / Michel Tremblay ; translated by
Sheila Fischman.

Translation of: La nuit des princes charmants.
ISBN 0-88922-510-9

    I. Fischman, Sheila II. Title. III. Title: Nuit des princes
charmants. English.

PS8539.R47N8413 2004   C843'.54
C2004-903259-3

The publisher gratefully acknowledges the financial support of the Canada
Council for the Arts; the Government of Canada through the Book
Publishing Industry Development Program; and the Province of British
Columbia through the British Columbia Arts Council for our publishing
activities.

In writing this story I've led some well-known personalities into a few adventures that are odd but always based on things that really happened. I hope they will take it with humour and that they'll forgive me.

For Gordon, whom I still run into on the street or at the theatre but never dare to approach, strictly out of shyness.

"Alas," said Candide, "I have known that love, the sovereign of our hearts, the soul of our soul; it has never brought me anything but one kiss and twenty kicks in the ass."

—Voltaire, *Candide*

PREAMBLE

Everything is in place. The third act is well underway, the characters—Mimi, Rodolfo, Marcello—have had time to situate us in the action: Mimi's cough is getting worse and worse, Rodolfo maintains that he wants to abandon her, Marcello is caught between them—eternal confidant of two lovers who adore but can't stand one another, the music stirs it all up in slow rhythms that make my head sway from right to left. I close my eyes at the very first measures. I don't need the libretto, I know it by heart.

On the brand-new turntable purchased by mail order, which my oldest brother spent a week assembling, Victoria de Los Angeles, Jussi Bjoërling and Robert Merrill are singing their hearts out and I'm spellbound.

Slumped in the big leatherette armchair, hands clasped over the early signs of a paunch that for the past few months has been a subject of mirth in my family—as adolescence ends and adulthood begins, I'm more attracted to chocolate cookies and Nestlé's Quik than to walks in the fresh air or physical exercise—I'm waiting for the great moment.

It's coming, it will happen in a few seconds; keeping my hands together, I raise them slowly and bring them close to my heart. Will the miracle happen again? Will I feel once more that incredible sense of sinking into the red leatherette as if my body has become a boat that's too heavy on a sea that's too small? Ecstasy, or something approaching it, always happens, always, every time; never has my soul not taken flight while my body was being imprinted on the fake leather, but every time I fear that I won't feel anything, that I've reached a saturation point where a single listening, the one too many—something else having grabbed my attention, some burning problem that stirs my blood and interferes with my concentration—will spoil forever the pleasure I've had from listening to this scene nearly every day now for such a long time.

Rodolfo has just confessed that he was guilty of bad faith, that he doesn't really want to abandon Mimi, that he will love her unto death, but that he's afraid because ...

Here it is.

Mimi è tanto malata!

The strings, especially the cellos that sound like hearts beating in slow motion, the heart-breaking melody I can't get out of my mind, that sometimes keeps me awake nights—Mimi, hidden behind the Gate of Hell, who learns that she is going to die; Rodolfo's despair; the anxiety of Marcello who is aware of Mimi's stupor, her dread: all that music at once sickly and energetic and amazingly effective, superimposed on a melodrama which is actually quite ordinary—all those flowing sounds that are intended to please, with no complexes, no shame—transport me yet again to that region of myself where I wish I could stay forever: the comfort of the waking dream.

The trio wraps itself around me, I wallow in it, I live with great delight the three tragedies that unfurl in my ear at the same time, I can live three of them simultaneously, I think that's it, that's what I like most of all.

Usually when I listen to this scene, I don't identify with any of the three characters in particular. I'm not one of those opera lovers who dreams of being Maria Callas suffering at the feet of Giuseppe di Stefano, or Renata Tebaldi grappling with the villain, Tito Gobbi, no, nothing makes me imagine myself as Floria Tosca plunging the knife into the breast of the sombre Scarpia, or as Salome who insists on kissing the mouth of the severed head of John the Baptist or as Lucia di Lamermoor outdoing herself as she spirals into trills during her improbable mad scene ... I'm not at all inclined to identify more with the female characters than the others; usually I'm the character who sings along if I like what he's singing—you should see me gesticulating with my cape during the toreador's aria or levitating into the Ceylonese night as I tackle Nadir's aria from *The Pearl Fishers*—and all at the same time during the ensembles—the joy of splitting yourself in four while listening to the second-last act of *Rigoletto*, or in seven during the denunciation scene in *Lucia*! I'm even the conductor when the most beautiful preludes and intermezzi burst out or—more rarely but still—a mute character who witnesses with sadistic joy the woes of others.

But I'm never in the chorus. A man's got his pride after all! Choruses are the only operatic pieces I listen to from the outside, staying in my chair while inside my head I'm *watching* a scene rather than living it as if I were one of the protagonists. I like listening to choruses, I don't like experiencing them.

Mimi, Rodolfo and Marcello interweave their heart-rending trio and I'm at the pinnacle of joy. The things I have to sing, I mean the words, are stunningly banal, so I put my entire soul into the music, and all at once my heart collapses into the sorrow of the failed painter who sees a couple, who are his friends, come undone before his eyes.

I experience two or three minutes of sheer ecstasy. The miracle has happened again, thank you Signor Puccini.

The trio ends, Marcello leaves the other two because he has just heard the voice of his beloved and oh so frivolous Musetta whom I really can't stand, who knows why, and my attention is somewhat disrupted by a thought that has just struck me. I leave Jussi and Victoria to their reunion so I can concentrate on the brand new embryonic thought which—I can sense—could assume great importance in my life if I dwell on it.

I have not yet really loved anyone. I nearly died of love when Marlon Brando ripped off his dirty T-shirt, crying, "Stella! Stella!" and I had a brief crush on Burt Lancaster in *Trapeze*, but I have not yet truly loved—and I often wonder, with a frown on my face and fear in my heart, when it will start, where I will be, with whom it will be and how it will happen ...

As I'm the only homosexual in my group, I don't know where to go to meet others and my terrible shyness keeps me from finding out. I often tell myself that sitting in the red armchair listening to Leonie Rysanek sing "The Willow Song" isn't liable to help me find my kindred spirit. There's Parc Lafontaine of course for the body's ecstasy, but that's just impersonal fondling that has nothing to do with any sentiment whatsoever. But I can't decide to make the big leap, to go off in search of adventure—or at least in search of others like me; I've been content with sublimating for too long as it is, I'm well aware of it and there's nothing I can do.

Sublimation is all well and good, but I'm starting to be a little bit over the hill to dream that Jean Besré is dying with love for me, or that Guy Provost is burying me under tons of the rarest and most fragrant flowers. That little theatre is no longer enough to fill my life or to satisfy my need for love.

Listening to the third act of *La Bohème* that day, I make myself a promise that brings some colour to my cheeks and a contented smile to my lips. It's still a dream, of course, but I sense that it's the final way out before I take the plunge, one last fantasia as my mother would say, before the real thing, and I wallow in it with obvious complacency.

I always say to everyone, especially to people who detest it, that what I like about opera is that nothing is realistic, ever—for the simple reason that everything is *sung*. It is perfect theatre, total transposition: everything is permitted because everything is absurd and everything is absurd because everything is sung. It's absurd to sing sublimely for fifteen minutes with a dagger in your chest as Riccardo does in *Un Ballo in Maschera*, or shut up in a potato sack like Gilda at the end of *Rigoletto*, or as poor Mimi does while she's dying of a lung disease! But often the beauty of opera is due in fact to the presence of the music, because what's being sung is really idiotic ... We pardon music for things that we'd never allow in spoken words, we cling to sensations that the music brings us rather than to the meaning of what's being sung; we let ourselves drift into feeling rather than thinking.

Actually, opera gives us permission to enjoy bad taste! Do the chic connoisseurs of Bayreuth and La Scala—the most snobbish, most discriminatory trash in the world— do they know that they have the most appalling bad taste? I often think about them and it breaks me up every time.

And so with that sense of derision that's been mine since childhood, my way of always transposing what doesn't suit me—sorrows, punishments, setbacks of every sort, experiencing them through culture instead of reality so that I don't really suffer, it occurs to me—very likely because I'm afraid of the first love that could light on me at any moment—to love while singing. Just like in an opera!

I see myself declaring my love to another guy while chirping a magnificent aria, rich with rhyme and well-placed tonic accents, in a setting that's a little ridiculous but not too much, bathed in lighting designed by a great artist, and dressed as I'd never dare to be in real life: somewhere between Medieval and Renaissance, tight and colourful ... This transposition of what I most desire in the world without having the courage to seek it out removes my inhibitions, and while the fourth act of Puccini's opera unfurls, I topple without realizing it into a terrifically soothing psychological striptease: I pass slowly from the

Middle Ages to the modern era, from tights to jeans, from puffy shirt to T-shirt, from a highly-polished setting to the sad reality of the one I live in, and for the first time in my life I try to imagine what my first boyfriend will look like. But—the final thread that holds me to my dream, the ultimate way of clinging to the absurd—I go on singing.

Yes, when I fall in love, I'll fall in love to music!

DOES PRINCE CHARMING EXIST?

I was eighteen, I was a virgin, and I'd had enough of sublimating as I dreamed in my bed about inaccessible beings, or groping in the shadows of parks fleeting bodies that were there not for love, but for the little death which is so short-lived and can be so sad when it's not accompanied by any sentiment. I had not yet experienced love in its classic array—creaking bed, the lengthy heavy breathing, the wrinkled sheets, the smell of the bodies before, during and after, the post-coital cigarette, the next date solicited shaking with the fear of being turned down—and I told myself it was high time I made up my mind to take the plunge.

In addition, it was winter, a rather slack season for practitioners of bucolic celebrations beneath the stars, and I had a powerful craving. The snow that was never removed was as much as six or eight feet high in Parc Lafontaine, the paths were often impassable, the nights too cold, and padded winter clothes not really suitable for quick unzipping. Besides, love in the snowbanks has never been my style.

As for the bars whose virtues I heard about now and then from a cruising partner chattier than the others, I was far too shy to go there, positive that the moment I set foot inside the Tropical or the Quatre Coins du Monde, both of them in the west end of town, which was still the preserve of Montreal Anglophones, dozens of heads would turn in my direction and grimaces of disgust would spread through the bar at the sight of the vulgar incarnation of the east end that I was: "What the hell is that?", "Good God, they let the uglies out tonight!", "How about that—it's the East End Bunny!" and so on.

So I continued to sublimate. So much that even Marlon Brando and Burt Lancaster lost their erotic interest, like old acquaintances you see too often.

I had to gather up my courage then, as much as I could on a Saturday night, then get dressed to kill—tight pants, black turtleneck, medallion on a leather thong around my neck, winter boots without too many salt stains—then hop on a bus and head directly for one of those *louche* bars—as they were still called at the time—without thinking about my complexes or my worries. Good luck, it's all in God's hands, break a leg and to hell with the consequences!

Between intention and realization, though, several weeks went by as I mused about Marlon in his T-shirt that got dirtier and dirtier and Burt greedily French-kissing Deborah Kerr in the storm-tossed waves of the Pacific. All that time, of course, Deborah Kerr was decked out in a lovely tire around her waist, her bathing suit didn't have a top and she sported a Roman haircut as well as the beginning of a most becoming mustache ... But when Marlon replaced me in Burt's arms and I caught myself mentally unwindng a porn filmI was no longer part of, I told myself I'd have to make up my mind before I went totally passive or lost all interest in anything that wasn't the product of my imagination.

Life, real life, was going to begin and I was dying of stage-fright. Would I be up to it? Would he? Would he transport me to seventh heaven or would he make me long for those sessions—which were more or less satisfying—in Parc Lafontaine and in my own bed? And what about me—would I even know what to do?

A rather circuitous way to inaugurate my dissolute life turned up around the middle of January. I was thrilled though I had no idea that this outing was going to take me into the twists and turns of worlds I didn't even know existed.

*

I was absent-mindedly leafing through *Le Petit Journal* as I always did on Saturday, lingering over the silliest stories or Louise Cousineau's gossip column, when I noticed an interview with Pierrette Alarie. I'd actually just finished listening to the Deutsche Grammophon disk she'd recorded with her husband, Léopold Simoneau, devoted to French opera duets. Both singers had quickly become my idols and I'd driven my family crazy for weeks with the duet from *The Pearl Fishers* and the bell song from *Lakmé*.

Madame Alarie announced that a few weeks later she was going to sing Juliet in Gounod's *Romeo and Juliet*, at Her Majesty's theatre, along with the American Richard Cassily and a glittering array of other Canadian singers, including Fernande Chiocchio, Napoléon Bisson, Gaston Gagnon and Claude Létourneau. She promised it would be an outstanding production with extravagant sets, colourful costumes, impassioned singing—in a word, an important event in Montreal's cultural life that it would be a crime to miss ...

Of Gounod all I knew was the inevitable *Faust*, which had been a passion during my adolescence: ah, the final trio with Victoria de Los Angeles, Nicolaï Gedda and Boris Christoff! I didn't even realize that he'd composed a *Romeo and Juliet*. This news put me in a state of delirious excitement: at last, I would have a chance to hear one of my idols in the flesh, in a real operatic production. An opera that I didn't even know! I raced through the article, looking for the ticket prices. They weren't given. Nervously I turned the cultural pages ... Surely there must be an ad for them somewhere ... Good God! They cost three dollars and fifty cents—an exorbitant amount for me, but this time I refused to be content with a ninety-cent student ticket at the very back of the second balcony or the end of a front row in the orchestra, where you see everybody in profile. This was going to be my first live opera and there was no way I was going to be jammed into an uncomfortable seat way up in the gods, with my knees crammed into the seat ahead of me and an uninterrupted view of the floor of the stage and the heads of the singers.

My mother advanced me the money, griping a little: "Good thing I've stopped keeping track of what you owe me because you'd be paying me back for the rest of your life!" And I was off to Her Majesty's.

At the time I was in my first year at the Institut des Arts Graphiques, destined not from choice but from sheer laziness, to go into printing, like my father and my brother, without yet knowing which aspect of it. The first year served as an introduction to printing: we checked out the various specializations and then, at the beginning of the second year, came the time to make our final choice. So far, the trades that we studied—typography and presswork —were very depressing, but I didn't dare say so to my parents, who were both so happy that I'd opted for a trade that September instead of going around announcing that I wanted to be a writer as I'd been doing in recent years. I still wanted to write but I had realized that I'd have to make my living too.

To make some spending money, I'd been a barbecued chicken delivery boy for four years; I'd been replaced—this is the absolute truth—by a fleet of trucks, as the restaurant dreamed of competing with the already all-powerful Saint-Hubert Barbecue. No more criss-crossing the streets of Plateau Mont-Royal on foot—Rachel to Saint-Grégoire, Amherst to Frontenac—arms loaded with shopping bags smelling of roast chicken and spicy sauce, now I had to think big, aim high! It didn't work: the trucks sat in the lane for several months, then disappeared overnight, but they didn't call me back. Once again I was sponging off my parents while I watched the new delivery boy—at least they'd given him a bike, lucky him—walk past the house, gasping like an old steam engine. Travelling the streets of Montreal on a bike in January was no laughing matter and I felt genuinely sorry for him.

I tried not to spend too much money, but my taste for everything cultural—films, books, theatre, records—ended up costing my mother a lot, she who held the purse-strings like a mama bear watching over her cubs.

For instance, I wanted to buy a book.

"Another one! You bought one last week!"

"I finished it."

"What will you do with it? At least when you used to go to the library you took them back and we never saw them again. But now they're all over the place and what am I supposed to do with them?"

"You read some of them ... "

"Sure, but when I'm finished they're in my way. Your brother's bookcase is already full, I don't know where to put them! Couldn't you sell them—or rent them!"

"Mama—for heaven's sake!"

But she always gave in, preferring to see me reading, I imagine, or going to the movies, even if it cost her plenty, than to see me smoking or drinking beer.

That morning, then: "Three-and-a-half dollars to see an opera! That's what your records cost and you can keep them forever."

"My records cost more than that ... "

"I know they do, four dollars and twenty-five cents! Honestly! Don't argue with me over seventy-five cents!"

"You always say my records are in your way."

"It's not your records, it's those books of yours that get in my way."

"Isn't it the same thing? Anyway, my records take up a lot more space than my books."

"They get used more too! When you finish a book you put it aside. But those damn opera records of yours ... Don't you ever get sick and tired of always listening to the same singers bleating the same stupid songs all day long?"

"Let's not start that again, Mama!"

"That opera of yours—when it's over you won't have anything!"

"You tell us about movies you saw twenty-five years ago, you still cry when you talk about *Since You Went Away* and *I Remember Mama*, so why can't I do the same thing with an opera?"

"If I'd known you were going to keep harping at me for twenty-five years with that opera, kiddo, I wouldn't have given you a cent!"

Another zany argument that wouldn't go anywhere. I let her rant away and finally she took out her transparent, powder-blue, plastic purse trimmed with silk flowers that had gone yellow in the sun.

"You're going to pay it all back when you start working, by the way ... "

"When I start working, Mama, you'll be the most pampered mother in creation!"

"Yeah, sure ... but I'll be too old to enjoy it!"

*

Instead of making Montrealers happy, the mild spell that had arrived the night before—with its melted snow and puddles, the dangerous icicles that were forming all over town—gave that Saturday afternoon, even though it was sunny, an odd little taste of a tragedy brewing, of a simmering disaster. No one was in the mood to run around shouting, "It's spring! It's spring!" as they do at the beginning of March when the snow really does melt and a promise of mildness is emerging in the west. Everybody was cursing, their feet wet and frozen, their behinds damp because falls were not uncommon, and their coats half-undone because of the suspect warmth that was more apt to be hiding a flu virus than a real foretaste of spring. We knew it was just a reprieve, a hypocritical day that could very well end with rain or a blustery wind, and we refused to be taken in by the slightest little particle of hope. For Montrealers, January—this was irreversible—would always mean despair.

Only the children enjoyed it: snowballs went flying in every direction, piles of red, blue or green rags dropped from balconies, accompanied by shouts from tearful adults who had done the same thing twenty years earlier: "Maurice, you're going to kill yourself!" "Come inside, Raymond, come back inside before you get crippled for life!" "Yike! How do you keep from getting dizzy? Jump from the *third* floor like that—you're crazy!" With snotty noses, wide-open eyes and wet mittens, the youngest kids envied the older ones who were brave enough to jump from such a height into the melting snowbanks. Ah, the dizziness! Ah, the excitement!

"Can I go too?"

"Are you nuts? You're so little you'd bounce!"

My feet were wet before I'd even boarded the first bus. I tried to walk in other people's footsteps but they all filled up with thick, icy water that got into even the best-lined boots and froze your woollen socks in half a second.

The bus smelled of wet dog, wet coats were dripping onto the floor, the windows were fogged over, the driver was in a foul mood and yelled at everybody, there were too many passengers squeezed in too tightly, complaining about the slow service, about the city, which didn't clear the snow fast enough, about the mayor who was more interested in the parties he gave than in his fellow citizens who were freezing to death because of his scandalous neglect. We'd elected him for days like this, not for useless commemorations or empty speeches!

St. Catherine Street was blocked in both directions; a bottleneck had formed going west from Bleury, and I had to walk the rest of the way—a half-hour of hell spent wading in slush and cursing my love of opera.

I could have phoned, reserved a seat, said that I'd pick up my ticket a few days later, but I wanted to hold it in my hand, put it in a safe place, look at it whenever I wanted, show it to my friends to get on their nerves, especially Pierre Morrissette who'd also gone through an opera phase, maybe copying me, maybe because he genuinely liked it.

I lingered in front of every movie theatre along the way—the Princess, the Palace, the Cinéma de Paris, the Loew's, the Seville—as much to warm my feet as to look at the posters. At the Seville, Sophia Loren and Charlton Heston were kissing passionately in front of a panorama of scorching desert, lucky them! I had seen *El Cid* a few weeks earlier and been bored to death, but now, with my icy feet and the soaking-wet hem of my pants, positive that a killer cold was being concocted somewhere in the vicinity of my sinuses, I was tempted to buy a ticket and spend three hours gazing at Spanish landscapes and the blazing desert sand. To hell with Rodrigue and Chimène, I want heat!

For me, St. Catherine Street west of Peel was an unfathomable mystery that I had not yet tried to solve. Throughout my childhood I hadn't even known that Anglos existed, that Montreal was divided in two, with the east end belonging to us Francophones and the west to the Anglos, that there was a conflict between the two solitudes, as we used to say, a conflict dating back to the Conquest in 1760 and that it was doubtful we'd ever see a way out of it, bad faith often prevailing in both camps and keeping the two sides from truly communicating.

For a long time I'd thought it strange that there were two Santas, one, Francophone at Dupuis Frères, the other, Anglophone, at Eaton's. Every December my mother took me to meet both of them and I asked each one for the same presents, in French, suspecting that the second didn't understand me, grateful to my mother though for translating *train électrique, poupées à découper, jeux de blocs* and *livres d'images.*

My nationalism was due among other things to how hard it was—the minute I'd crossed the frontier of St. Lawrence Boulevard—to go to movie theatres in the west end, to be served in French in my own city. On this abnormally mild January afternoon, infuriated by my wet clothes and sure I was coming down with a monstrous flu, I felt sorry for anyone who refused to speak to me in my language.

When I got to Her Majesty's I was shaking all over and chilled to the bone.

A small line-up stretched into the lobby, all young men not much older than me, except for an aging lady at the box office who had a lot of trouble pronouncing the name of Pierrette Alarie, whom she didn't know and whose pedigree she requested of the poor cashier I could see gesticulating impatiently.

All the young men turned in my direction and ...

The insistent looks, the languid way they stood, the clothes, so different from those usually worn by the people I knew but that I would have chosen myself if I'd been left alone in the menswear section of a big department store ...

My God!

So I wasn't the only man in Montreal to go through a Robert Merrill phase. And I'd landed in a nest of worshippers.

I'm pretty sure I turned red all of a sudden, in any event I started looking for my money, head down, chin pushed into my scarf to hide my embarrassment as I tried to look composed. I took my place in line, making myself as small as I could. Did my clothes proclaim my plebeian roots? Did I still smell of the leftover pea soup I'd eaten so greedily before I left the house? Was the pompom on my tuque too big?

The old lady was still asking questions; I couldn't hear what the ticket-seller was saying over the irritated sighs of the young men who were using the occasion not only to express their impatience but also to talk to each other without appearing to be cruising. They were probably there for the same reason I was, but would never admit it even under torture.

The one just ahead of me—I immediately christened him International Festival of Freckles—turned in my direction for the second time, with an amused little smile that appealed to me right away.

"Honestly! She doesn't even *know* who Perrette Hallery *is!*"

Perrette Hallery?

I tucked my giggles into the collar of my coat, which I hadn't unbuttoned yet. But I was sure that my ears were blazing red, they felt so hot and throbbing.

"*You* know who she is, don't you? Perrette Hallery?"

I heard myself say a feeble "yes" in reply and immediately felt terrible. I wasn't going to start talking English just because a redhead who was just a little too good-looking deigned to speak to me.

"You're French, aren't you?"

"Yes." (Again!)

"And you're laughing because I don't pronounce her name right?"

"No, no ... "

"How do *you* pronounce it?"

I brought out my finest accent, careful to avoid rolling my *rs*, that indisputable proof of the lower-class Montrealer, and said: "Pierrette Alarie."

"That's very different from what I said ... "

"Yes, it is ... "

"You love her?"

"Maddely."

"Not *maddely*, madly. Two syllables, not three. Now we're even ... "

The old lady trotted by us. She spoke to the handsome redhead as if she knew him.

"I wish the Opera Guild would produce operas with *real* singers, not *locals!*"

All heads turned in her direction and the young man who was paying for his ticket snapped:

"Lady, Perrette Hallery is one of the best opera singers in the world!"

This time, it was pride that made me blush and I grew a good inch taller.

So they did have some taste after all!

The old lady shrugged as she left. In her opinion this city certainly couldn't possibly produce one of the world's greatest opera singers; all it had was puddles of slush and horrible flu.

The customers in line knew what they wanted: the performance, the price, the end of the row or the middle, sometimes even the precise seat. Once they'd bought their tickets, though, they stuck around the lobby, pretending to check their change or study the posters for upcoming productions, on the lookout and—of this I was sure—with hearts pounding.

Would someone talk to them or would they have to wait till the night of the performance for someone finally to approach them?

One couple had already formed, a pair of extremely ugly pimple-faced pansies who, as soon as they'd introduced themselves and shaken hands, had launched into a competition over recording dates, who sang with whom, when and where—suddenly animated, less inclined to cruise than to show off their knowledge, happy to find at last if not the kindred spirit, then at least a close relation. All I could hear was Callas, Callas, Callas, and I shook my head a little. Grow up guys; look elsewhere, open your souls, don't lock yourselves away in the narrow idolatry of a single vestal virgin, no matter how brilliant she is! I wanted to talk to them, teach them, praise Leonie Rysanek or Birgit Nillson or my beautiful Victoria de Los Angeles, but I knew it would be rude and pointless: they'd recognized each other, each thought the other interesting, they were already talking about going for a coffee, and good for them! I was actually close to envying the way they'd connected so easily even though they were uglier than me.

My speckled redhead bought two tickets and I found myself trying to guess what the guy who'd go with him would look like ... Another redhead? A bland blond? Then I felt a little ashamed of my narrow-mindedness, of the facile clichés my imagination tended to come up with, and tried to imagine my redhead with ... with ... But he added, turning his head slightly so I could hear him—at least that's what I thought he was doing:

"Yes, first row, please. My mother has trouble with her eyes ... But not in the centre ... "

He was bringing his mama!

I could already see Maureen O'Hara make her entrance into Her Majesty's on her son's arm; they came towards me: introductions, expensive heady perfume, emerald-green gown, of course, with a neckline that plunged so low it was scary, devastating smile, sensual voice.

"My son told me you were cute, but I never thought ... "

A little tap on the shoulder brought me back to reality. I was alone at the wicket, the cashier was giving me a strange look. My redhead had gone. I turned around to look for him. There was a line-up behind me again—a dozen more or less young men who were getting impatient, two elderly Madames—sisters, I was sure, their hats complemented each other so well, a bald priest who'd taken the initiative and tugged me out of my daydream by telegraphing his intentions with an unambiguous smile— but Perrette Hallery really had vanished.

The idyll had been very brief!

I leaned over towards the ticket-seller, nearly froze the tip of my nose on the glass that was still cold despite the heating which couldn't get rid of the prevailing dampness in the theatre lobby.

"One ticket for the 26th, please. The best one you've got."

The cashier hesitated briefly, then told me rather stupidly: "You can talk French to me you know, it's allowed!"

I heard snickering behind me.

Shame is a sentiment we don't experience only during great humiliations; it often springs up, stinging and oppressive, at inconsequential, unexpected moments, when your vulnerability, disarmed, is most sensitive, and your fighting spirit at zero. At such times it paralyzes you, leaves you speechless, your mind blank, drained and miserable.

Drained and miserable I was in front of the pretty ticket-seller I'd have given hell to had she dared speak to me in English and who was absolutely right to chew me out. With red ears and quivering chin (hey, come on, you're eighteen years old, you aren't a child, grin and bear it, you know how to defend yourself), I stammered my order in a language that was closer to baby talk than to the clear, precise expression of an adult brain. I paid quickly, pocketed my ticket, and made a mad dash for the theatre door without a look at the line-up where I was positive that a dozen homosexuals—including a priest—each one a bigger bitch than the others, would laugh at my disappointment.

I wasn't in the habit of analyzing my behaviour, of racking my brains to pin down my reasons for doing what I'd done or saying what I'd said, but on my way out of Her Majesty's that day, when I plunged back into the cold air, the cold water, the dirt on Guy Street and the fractious crowd, I couldn't help calling myself every terrible name I could think of—of which *traitor* was far from the worst.

All it took was for a cute Anglo to take an interest in me and right away I laid down my arms without even asking if he understood a word of French! Because it was easier, simpler, because I knew, actually, I didn't need to ask him, I'd been forced to learn *his* language, but he hadn't had to learn mine. And that if I'd answered him in French, probably he'd have lost interest.

I was so humiliated I could have slapped myself. So I was willing to do anything to keep someone interested in me?

My only hope was that Perrette Hallery and Maureen O'Hara wouldn't be at the same performance as me.

Then an idea started running through my head: he'd said a ticket in the first row ... but not in the centre ... Was that his way of apologizing for having bought two ninety-cent tickets—student tickets, poor people's tickets? That made him even more likable, and for the second time in half an hour, I forgot my nationalist impulses; but this time it was to switch over to an erotic daydream in which Burt and Marlon were replaced by a shock of red hair, myriad freckles, and the beginning of a paunch.

*

My ticket for *Romeo and Juliet* didn't impress my friends, not even Pierre Morrissette who simply said, arching his eyebrows slightly to make sure I saw his contempt:

"You spent three-and-a-half bucks to see that! Everybody says it's the pits! Why d'you think it's never performed? You should wait for the Metropolitan Opera tour. They know how to sing! And they sing things you want to hear!"

"But they come to the Forum! You can't hear a note there, it's so big and there's so much echo!"

"Doesn't matter, I'd rather hear good singers not very well than bad ones properly!"

Pure jealousy? Could be, but I'd made an impression; I stuffed my ticket back in my pocket, telling myself: "It's going to be good, it's going to be good, and I'll piss him off so badly when I tell him how good it was, he'll never recover. Because I'll never miss a chance to remind him. Besides, even if it's as bad as he says, I'll still say it was fantastic, just to make him sick!"

Reading another interview with Pierrette Alarie, this one in *La Presse*, I realized a few days later that there would be just one performance of *Romeo and Juliet*, when I'd thought there would be four or five. So Montreal didn't have enough opera lovers to fill Her Majesty's more than once? And judging by the ones I'd seen at the box office, next Saturday would I be in the company of a few elderly ladies and some pretty gentlemen? It was liable to be very interesting ...

So Perrette and his mother would be there at the same time as me. I could find out if Maureen really existed or if Red had used her as an alibi—as I tended to believe more and more—to conceal at the same time his lack of money and the existence of a guy in his life.

As for my family's reactions, they were predictable and not in the least surprising: my mother heaved a long sigh that she meant to be guilt-inducing, but that I allowed to roll off me as if I hadn't heard her; my father, who of course would have preferred it if I'd waved around a ticket for a hockey game, merely said that a few years earlier, Her Majesty's had been known as His Majesty's (I knew that! After all, I was ten when Princess Elizabeth became Queen!); my brother repeated Pierre Morrissette's remarks practically word for word, but added: "Where'd you get the money to pay for that ticket? More waste! I don't give Mama money every week for theatre tickets, it's to pay for your education!"

But I refused to be demoralized by sarcasm or to feel guilty because I'd spent three dollars and fifty cents for a show, and I stood there with my ticket for *Romeo and Juliet* which, after all, I'd originally planned to be a cover for my first adventure into Montreal-by-night's places of ill-repute, which I wanted to get to know; the opera would end late, I would already be in the west end, and I'd decided that come Saturday night, I'd be bold enough to go inside the doors of the mysterious world of the brotherhood I knew I belonged to, but that filled me with apprehension because I didn't know how to approach it.

*

The week was long, especially because, thanks to my impatience, my courses at the Institut des Arts Graphiques seemed even duller and more second-rate than usual. I entered the smell of the printshop at eight-thirty a.m. and didn't leave until four, dazed, often anxious, and with the impression that I'd wasted my day in front of a litho press whose functioning I'd never figure out, or feigning attention during general knowledge classes—French, math, and so on—less advanced than the ones I'd taken the year before in high school; I wasn't learning anything about the trade I'd decided to practise and I'd be demoted in the subjects I could have excelled at.

I had not yet made any friends in that school where, in any case, I felt like some external element, a foreign body that didn't belong there, and I spent my lunch hours alone, standing at a window, munching on a ham or chicken sandwich or, on Friday, one made of chopped stuffed olives and Cheez Whiz, the best treat of all, which had just come into my life and still makes my mouth water when I think about it. I didn't step outside the school because it was too cold—in fact, I didn't once set foot in the school-yard during my three years at the institute, even when it was mild—I read novels, I did my homework, I stargazed ... That hour and a half of freedom seemed almost as long to me as the endless classes that came before and after.

It's not surprising then that he heroes of operas and their implausible adventures fascinated me so much during that particularly dreary period of my life. Through them I experienced some impossible imbroglios: I'd spent more than a month untangling the plot of *Il Trovatore* and I still wondered why Renato in *Un Ballo in Maschera* didn't recognize his wife when he was bawling a duet with her that went on for a quarter of an hour; even though she was veiled, surely the fat soprano must have at least looked familiar! I became by turns an Egyptian princess, a French slut, an Italian poet, Babylonian king, Irish lover, Spanish barber, loathsome child, wicked witch, Roman patriot, Celtic priestess; I lived anywhere at all except Montreal, in every era except my own, in every layer of society save the one I'd been born in (printers are a rare commodity in opera); I howled my unhappy loves loud enough to snap my vocal chords and I imagine it consoled me for my non-existent loves.

When my mother saw me come home from school around five, she didn't ask about my day, she merely said:

"If you play your music too loud again, I'm calling the police, I'll tell them I don't know you, that you're a roomer who's making a noise, that I've told you five hundred times and I don't know how to kick you out."

She was joking, but barely. She'd never called the police but she threatened to countless times unless I made Salomé or Don Giovanni turn it down. Or, worst of all, because she really hated Wagner's music, Brunhilda or Isolde. When once again the house was filled with "Ritorna vincitor" from *Aida*, or the "Habanera" from *Carmen*, she'd storm into my room without knocking, lift the arm off the turntable, bring both hands to her heart and shriek: "If I hear that one more time I'll blow up and it'll take three days to pick up the pieces!"

I'd put on another record, an opera she didn't know or one of the less thundering Haydn symphonies, she would calm down and go back to the dining room, and barely fifteen minutes later Carmen would proclaim once more that love is a rebellious bird which nobody can tame ...

*

At last the great day arrived, as they say in the fairy tales.

The freezing rain had gone on for most of the week, the sidewalks gleamed like skating rinks, and the trees were corseted in very beautiful but very treacherous ice—on melting it exploded into stinging rain that was almost like hail; branches broken off cleanly and even a few tree trunks littered the streets—and the streets themselves, awash in a mixture of cold water and ice, were nearly impassable. In a word you had to really want to hear *Romeo and Juliet* to venture out that night. And I did!

I had a problem though: what to wear? You don't dress like a bum for the opera, of that I was sure, and everything I owned reeked hopelessly of poverty and hand-me-down. First I tried on what looked "cleanest," an old suit of my

older brother's that my mother had got altered by someone who obviously didn't know a thing about it and then
dyed it midnight blue which didn't fool anybody: the traces
of wear at the elbows and knees were more apparent than
ever. Wearing a threadbare suit when you're eighteen years
old is a mortification that's hard to bear. The pants were
too big around the waist, the jacket too narrow in the
shoulders, and worst of all, one pocket was coming
unstitched. No way was I going to appear before *le tout
Montréal* dressed like the poor cousin! Even though I was
nothing more than the poor cousin's poor cousin.

I pulled on some jeans—my mother was already in the
doorway, shouting that she wouldn't let me leave the
house to go to the opera dressed like a bum, even if I was
a consenting adult—and then I noticed the sexy pair of
black pants that I usually wore for my nocturnal roaming.
They were too light for the season, but they fit well, I felt
handsome in them: with a black turtleneck and my boat-
necked forest-green sweater, I'd rather look like an artist,
and I would rather look like an artist than a yokel.

To leave the house without my mother seeing my get-up,
however, I resorted to a trick that I thought very clever, but
that proved to be disastrous. I took my heavy winter coat to
my room, ostensibly to brush it—it was camel-hair from
an animal that had died of fright—and walked quickly past
Mama—buttons done up to the neck and the preoccupied
look of a person with a lot to do.

"Are you dressed at least decently?"

"Of course ... "

"Let me see ... "

"I haven't got time, I'll be late."

"You won't be late, it's so early they probably haven't put
up the sets yet."

"It's a long way, I need time to get there! I have to take
two buses and the weather's lousy!"

"Have you got on a shirt and tie at least?"

"Sure."

"Which tie?"

"The one you love, the ugly one."

"I don't believe you! Let me see how you're dressed."

"Mama, I'm eighteen years old, I've got the right to dress however I want!"

"Dress as you want, but don't try telling me you've got something on that you don't. I know you well enough to be pretty sure you aren't traipsing around in your winter coat for no reason!"

"Okay, you win. As usual."

I undid my coat and paraded in front of her in the dining room.

"Now are you happy?"

She didn't move a muscle but I could see the dismay in her eyes. She took a sip of tea, then shifted her attention to the TV set where Nicole Germain was telling her guests how to stay young and beautiful. About this kind of program Mama always said: "Those women have nothing to do but starve to death so they can fit into little girls' dresses!"

But she still followed their career with a dedication worthy of the most fanatic fans.

"You look stupid the way you like, it's fairly good, but there's one thing missing."

She'd spoken without looking at me while I was buttoning my coat.

"What do you mean, one thing missing?"

"Don't you usually wear that damn thing around your neck when you get all dressed up?"

She was right, I'd forgotten the final touch, the accessory that completed my artist's get-up: my marrowbone.

A few months earlier my mother had bought some marrowbones to make soup. Instead of beef, the butcher had given her veal; she complained a little, but put them into the boiling water anyway because it was too late to send the package back to Monsieur Longpré. Then finally she decided that it wasn't worth getting worked-up because—to her amazement—her soup ended up practically the same: the same texture, the same colour, and no greasier than usual.

At supper though she'd apologized a little when she served it, just in case—though it was unlikely—we caught her out.

"You're going to eat something different tonight ... I made my beef soup out of veal."

She was relieved when my father had a good laugh—for him, a spoiled soup was a personal insult that he took very badly, the meal was permanently ruined, and he'd sulk for most of the evening—but still she watched apprehensively as he swallowed his first spoonful.

"If you hadn't told me I'd never have known. It's delicious!"

When the dish was put down in front of me I was bowled over: not by the steaming soup that did in fact taste the same as what we ate every day, but for the pretty little veal bone, round and white and flat, that sat in the midst of the tomatoes and the elbow macaroni. I gnawed off the tiny filaments of meat that were still attached to it, then I put it beside my plate to dry. My mother frowned when she spotted it as she was clearing the table, but she said nothing, probably to avoid attracting my father's attention and my brother's wrath.

When we'd finished eating I took the little bone to the bathroom where I scraped it and brushed it to make it shine, then I left it to dry on the soap dish.

The next day, I ran a leather thong through the gleaming clean hole and wore it proudly that afternoon when a bunch of us went out to the movies or something else, I don't remember. I have to say, it looked terrific against my bottle-green sweater, and my admiring friends swore that they'd try to make one too the next time their family had soup for supper. Their mothers must have been stricter than mine—either that or their soups weren't as inspiring as my mother's—because I was still the only one with such a gorgeous pendant. I was very happy; I had no desire to be part of what was liable to be known in the neighbourhood as *the marrowbone gang*.

"Thanks, Mama, I'd forgotten!"

Leaving Nicole Germain to her advice, Mama looked at me.

"Did you think I was serious? You aren't going to wear that! You aren't going to the opera with a soup bone around your neck!"

"Why not?"

"I'm warning you, you aren't leaving my house with that thing around your neck! People will think you're a cannibal! Why not put one in your nose while you're at it! And a grass skirt! And rope sandals!"

"Mama, please! I'm all dressed, I'm ready to go, this is no time to start an argument that'll never end and will make me late!"

"You won't be late if you leave here without that soup bone, I can tell you that!"

"I'm not leaving here without it and I won't be late either! My marrowbone is part of my personal style and that's that!"

"His personal style! How about that! When people get a look at it they won't call it personal style, they'll bring out a straitjacket!"

"Oh sure! Everybody knows they've got straitjackets in every theatre in the world!"

"If it's people like you that go there, they darn well ought to."

"Mama ... I'm leaving now and don't try stopping me!"

With hand on heart—her ultimate trick to tell us we were breaking her heart when she didn't know what to say—she put on what I called, after seeing Marguerite Jamois at the Comédie Canadienne some years before, her Athalie look when telling about the horrors in the dead of night.

"Okay, have it your way. You always do anyway! Make a fool of yourself, somebody we know's going to see you and they'll phone me tomorrow to tell me that my own child struts around Her Majesty's with the supper leftovers hanging around his neck!"

I left the house without a word or we'd have been off for the evening, and the opera the two of us would improvise couldn't have been set to music by anyone.

*

Maureen O'Hara really did exist!

They arrived a few minutes after me, but I nearly missed them, lost as I was in contemplation of everything around me.

I was in the lobby watching the parade of opera lovers— women curled to the gums and bejewelled to the elbows; gentlemen in evening dress, visibly disheartened, who'd have given anything to be far away—at the nearby Forum, say, or in a private club, holding a newspaper while a cigar was burning away in a brass ashtray; it smelled of the bank, the Stock Exchange, and big business, not of love of culture; young girls tagging along behind their parents, buffed, currycombed, dragooned into coming to the opera by mothers who in the past had been figures in the carpet too, but had learned over time how to trample on them; and young men like me, opera aficionados, aware of their difference or not, who studied each new face, handsome or ugly, that appeared at the two front doors, in search of a sign of recognition, a gaze just the slightest bit persistent, maybe even a smile.

I myself fell in love every thirty seconds, convinced that this or that spectator—not always young, by the way, because men of a certain age were quite numerous and quite attractive—was looking my way, locking eyes with me, hesitating to approach me. In spite or because of my marrowbone.

I had really come to the right place!

Who knows, maybe I wouldn't have to go to the Quatre Coins du Monde after the show to lose what I'd come here to lose.

A few noisy conservatory students of music or theatre had gone past me laughing, very concerned about their appearance and very aware of their impact. Brazenly polyglot, the musicians, I assumed, were conversing in several languages: I'd heard French, English, Italian and German.

Every one was better-looking than the other: the girls in colourful clothes in tones I'd never seen on my girl cousins or friends—fuchsia, mauve, purple, rust, khaki; the guys decked out in bowler hats or Basque berets, scarves flung over one shoulder European-style, some with a pipe, others smoking cigarettes, laughing, impudent and oh so sexy! Young actors were reputed to be of my "orientation," so I tried to guess who was or wasn't ... I chose the best looking and had an intense ten-second affair with every one.

I was watching them all rush onto the stairs to the balcony when I spotted Perrette Hallery from behind, accompanied by a gorgeous woman with a monkey-fur coat, dramatically red hair under her veiled hat, milky skin and confident gait. The cliché of the beautiful Irishwoman, Maureen O'Hara come down from the screen to inject a little splendour into Montreal's tedious nightlife, Beauty visiting the Beasts.

The other women didn't wear their furs, they inhabited them; Maureen didn't even seem aware of the weight of hers as she tripped along blithely in her stiletto-heeled winter boots, the first I'd ever seen—unthinkable in this climate which was more suited for ugly boots than elegant shoes—but very real nonetheless.

The monkey fur followed each of her movements and gave her the allure of a flapper, attracting many admiring looks. All at once, the men had stopped wishing they weren't there, while the women shrugged in irritation, I could practically hear their harsh verdicts: "Look at that, here comes the Irish Slut!" But you could also hear them raging with jealousy.

Maureen was holding the arm of her son and I thought at first that she was blind. But she was looking around with the strange expression of the near-sighted who doesn't really see her surroundings and relies on vague outlines to guide herself. My redhead hadn't lied at the box office: his mother really did have trouble with her eyesight! So had I been wrong about him too, was he irrevocably heterosexual? No, I mean, really. No! In fact I had proof right away.

He must have spotted me in the lobby because he turned in my direction while the ticket-taker was busy tearing off stubs. Was it a real smile and should I smile back? If so, what kind of message should I send? Act surprised, glad, indifferent, not-in-the-least-interested even if I actually was a little bit? Or was I really? And how to translate into a smile that you're *a little bit* interested? In the time it took to analyze it all, Perrette and Maureen had disappeared into the house, which was abuzz with the murmurs of the local opera-fans and I stood there alone with the same stupid, impassive expression and the ticket stub in my hand.

First chance missed; I could have slapped myself!

It was eight twenty-five. The show was about to begin. Wilfrid Pelletier must be waiting in the wings to appear before his orchestra. The lobby of Her Majesty's now held only the lonely types like me who couldn't make up their minds to go inside, just in case ...

With all that, I'd forgotten why I was there. What awaited on the other side of the padded doors was more important than a parade of penguins and minks, or a smile wrenched off a face that was as desperate as mine.

Here's to us, Monsieur Gounod, and may the lovers of Verona move me deeply!

*

Maestro Wilfrid Pelletier must have been disappointed at the reception he was given. Polite, nearly indifferent applause greeted his entrance, he climbed onto the podium amid nearly total apathy but he still had his musicians stand, perhaps out of bravado, then turned to face the audience who weren't even looking in his direction; his fine, intelligent head bent just as silence was restored, and there he was bowing low to a crowd that was totally silent except for a few dry coughs from a few bored gentlemen.

Was that how Montreal celebrated her most famous conductor? Did the people to whom he had bowed even know who he was? I doubted it and I was furious. I would have gladly shouted *bravo*, shown my enthusiasm before this man who had, after all, directed at the Metropolitan Opera, and married Rose Bampton, a great diva, but I was too shy and I contented myself with suffering on his behalf, with sensing his humiliation, his inner rage in front of a house full of ignoramuses.

Then I thought about the conservatory students who weren't giving him a triumphant welcome either. Revenge of students against their master, silent protest towards a hated teacher? But I didn't know whether Monsieur Pelletier taught at the Conservatory or not ... Was Wilfrid Pelletier a conductor people didn't respect and I didn't know? I'd always thought he was the idol of Montreal music-lovers, because of all he'd done for the symphony orchestra, for music on television. No, I chose to believe that the audience that night was ignorant and uncouth.

I looked around; no one seemed interested in what was going on in the pit. The women were fiddling with their flashy bracelets, the men were covering their eyes as a sign of concentration, but they weren't fooling anyone; you could practically hear them dreaming about odorous baby dolls or columns of numbers that kept growing longer ...

I had an excellent seat in the orchestra, in the middle of the ninth row. My marrowbone had caused a sensation when I took off my coat before slipping into the row of uncomfortable old seats, brown and gold if memory serves, their velvet upholstery threadbare. I didn't have the money for a coat check, so I was fated to sit through the opera buried under my heavy winter coat folded double that would dry on my knees, leaving a nasty feeling of dampness in my joints. If I turned arthritic at fifty it would most likely be due to the generations of coats that had dried on my knees. Unless I got rich.

I had pretended to be looking for my seat, craning my neck, knitting my brow, to give people a good look at my pendant. One lady said to her husband as I walked past them on the way to my seat: "Did you see that? He's wearing a bone!"

Her husband answered her in French, hurray for bilingualism: "He must've made a mistake. They'll send him to the second balcony and that'll be the last we see of him."

"Well," she told him in English, "I certainly hope so!"

Just as Maestro Pelletier turned around so the show could begin, the lady leaned across to her husband and told him—in French without a hint of English (so she was Francophone too!):

"He's still here."

The husband leaned towards me, which given his wife's impressive physique wasn't easy, and stared at me as if I'd just begged him for a dollar.

"If it's his seat he should have the decency to dress properly! You don't show up in the Queen's theatre dressed like a beggar!"

"He might be an artist."

"He's nobody!"

"He might be an *important* artist"

"Nobody's important at *that* age!"

His wife half rose:

"Change seats with me, I'm afraid he might be a beatnik!"

"We'll change at intermission or we'll disturb everybody. And he won't bite you, for Christ's sake!"

She sat down again, letting loose all around her a huge bubble of cheap perfume. It didn't smell of violets, it smelled of VIOLET. I brought my hand to my nose quite conspicuously, but she didn't seem to get the message.

"Anyway, if he smells I don't care if it disturbs Pierrette Alarie, we're moving!"

I'd produced my effect, I was pink with pleasure. I hoped that I'd even seriously ruined the pleasure of a nouveau riche couple who spoke English together in public so they'd think they had attained a certain status or a certain power in a society in which French was looked down on, but who switched to French automatically when they felt they were on the defence.

I almost wished that I did smell of beatnik—whatever that might be!

The spotlight that made Wilfrid Pelletier's white hair gleam went out abruptly, and just before I looked up at the stage where any minute now, Renaissance Verona would come to life (I didn't know yet that Gounod had concocted an excruciatingly boring prologue that goes on for six or seven minutes before the curtain rises on the Capulets' ballroom), during that fraction of a second when a theatre isn't altogether dark yet and you can still make out who is there, which individuals who don't know each other have come together to attend the most fascinating ceremony in the world, I caught a glimpse of a shock of red hair, wild and daunting in the very first row, far to the conductor's left, a flamboyant stain, a sign of life in the row of uniformly brown or blond North American heads, all clean and all styled by the same barber.

Imagine my stupor when the curtain went up on a Capulets' ballroom that looked more like a dungeon from Torquemada's Inquisition than the Borgias' Renaissance: squat, dimly lit, narrow, all fake towers and stained-glass windows made of mica, it was inhabited by a totally frozen crowd that didn't seem to be enjoying themselves despite what they were singing while they held papier mâché goblets: "L'heure s'envole, joyeuse et folle ... " They were far from wild, and joy had been totally banished. The chorus was there to work, not to have fun! And all those fine folk—the women in hennins that looked like dunce caps, the men decked out in strawberry pies made of velvet that sat on wigs as hard as pottery straight from the kiln—all those fine folk were watching Wilfrid Pelletier wide-eyed, wagging their chins in rhythm with his baton.

As a party, it was not a triumph!

Besides that, everything was blue and green, two colours I can't stand next to each other on a stage: if a chair had the misfortune to be green, its cushion and trim were blue; and if a drapery happened to be blue, both the cord holding it back and its pompom glowed in a lovely green, and so forth—every time. An appalling and nerve-wracking lack of imagination prevailed on the stage where one of the most beautiful love stories in the world was going to unfold, and I thought to myself, suffering in advance (one of my personal favourite flaws):

"If the balcony scene is green and blue, I'm walking out!"

I was even more stunned a few minutes later, after Papa Capulet's boring first aria, when I realized that the set was a carbon copy of the one for the first act of *Swan Lake* by the Royal Winnipeg Ballet that I'd seen in this same theatre a year before! The more I studied it the surer I was: it was smaller, like a twin brother who hasn't reached his normal height yet, but it was the same. To the point where I kept expecting to see Prince Siegfried in his jam-packed padded tights, accompanied by Odette or Odile squeezed into her featherless bird's costume ... Then I got it: it was exactly the same set, but for the ballet they'd simply pushed back the walls to provide more space for the dancers to do their thing.

Did Her Majesty's have a warehouse where they stored a single set for everything in the repertoire—ballet, opera, theatre—that was set between the year 1000 and the 19th century? And did the audience go along with it?

I looked at the lady beside me, so afraid that I might smell of beatnik when she was the one who smelled—of thousands of murdered flowers. Her bright eyes, her bright face, spoke eloquently and rapturously of her boundless happiness. She had never seen anything so beautiful in her whole life. Obviously she hadn't been able to drag her husband to *Swan Lake* the year before.

The first act was redeemed by Juliet's "Je veux vivre," which Pierrette Alarie sang wonderfully in her crystal-clear voice of a little girl who was over forty. (I could always pretend not to notice that she wasn't fourteen years old because she was excellent and tiny, but the unappealing physique of her obese Romeo—who was also a bad actor and the living, breathing cliché of an opera tenor—had me gnashing my teeth while the hair on my arms stood up.) To my amazement, the aria didn't get much applause and I was starting to wonder if the audience around me was actually alive. I glanced up at the balcony where the students and opera lovers would normally express their pleasure. Didn't they at least appreciate Pierrette's vibrato? I couldn't see them and they sat there in the shadows mute, like a reproach or worse, a threat. In fact they were right, but I was clinging to the last of my illusions because this was my first time at the opera, I'd been dreaming of it all week and it didn't have the right to be bad!

The rest of the act was miserably botched: the young lovers' first duet was as erotic as the meeting of a pair of raw filets of sole; Romeo's growing passion burned like an ice floe in January, his madrigal was executed like Marie-Antoinette on the Place de Grève, and the whole thing wound up with Papa Capulet urging everyone to go on partying.

Stupidity, mediocrity, letdown.

But just as Juliet's father came out with his ridiculous yet oh so relevant: "Autrefois, j'en fait serment, nous dansions plus vaillamment," repeated till we couldn't take it any more by a chorus more lethargic than ever—you could practically hear how anxious the chorus members were to quench their thirst at intermission—one of the bewigged faces around Romeo caught my eye, he was somewhere near the last column on the right, between the staircase lit in blue, needless to say, and a green drapery with gold stitching (it had the good fortune of not being blue).

He'd been spared the hat that looked like a strawberry pie, but was rigged out with a blond wig topped with a little royal-blue cap that clashed dramatically with his bushy black eyebrows. Along with the others he was singing "Le plaisir n'a qu'un moment; terminons la nuit gaiement!" though he didn't seem to know what he was doing on this stage, in the midst of a motionless crowd, drowned in green and blue adornments with guests who were bored even as they sang the contrary, to what sounded like kazoo music that would make anyone shiver. Arms dangling, shoulders hunched, tights ravelled at the knees, eyes glued on Wilfrid Pelletier as if he were the singer's last hope for survival, he looked so miserable that I felt a pang. An inexplicable burst of adrenaline, starting at my solar plexus and radiating through my whole body, overwhelmed me as if some great thing had just happened. Or something catastrophic.

Leaning to my right, I craned my neck a little to get a better look, and the woman next to me recoiled rather too obviously to be truly sincere.

My bewigged false blond followed the crowd's lead with particular clumsiness. How had I not spotted him before? Where had he been hiding? Unaccustomed to the stage, he could barely conceal his stage fright. Had his fellow singers pushed him reluctantly onto the boards, telling him he had to earn his keep like everybody else, that even an opera singer had to earn his fee?

But he was so handsome, so touching in his discomfort ... I didn't know if I was happy to observe him because I was moved by how ridiculous he looked, or if I shared his suffering at singing idiotic songs in an idiotic opera, surrounded by idiots dressed up as if they were starring in a carnival of the poor. I liked to think that he realized how petty and insignificant everything was around him on this stage, and that what he felt was shame at being part of it.

So Prince Charming did exist and he was dressed like a operetta pageboy in a bad operatic production!

I felt very hot during the final minute of the act, but now I didn't want the curtain to close on this appalling provincial production, I wanted to go on looking at the poor child (he seemed to be not much older than me) performing in the absurd world of the opera; I wanted to feel sorry for him, to go onstage and console him, protect him, embrace him, telling him: "Come on, I'll get you out of this, we'll be happy, you're already in a costume that makes me happy—but lose the wig!"

(I was the one on the white horse who would kidnap the little pageboy, his hair now curly and black, while singing an extremely beautiful aria, a unique bravura piece that all the baritones in the world would fight over for centuries to come ... The opera I was imagining surpassed everything I'd ever heard—in lyricism, but also in boldness: *Romeo and Romeo*, a parallel opera, an original work, on the fringes of everything that had been done to date ... an undeniable masterpiece, a combination of Puccini and Puccini, with a happy ending that would make you feel good and that would last a lifetime! All within sixty seconds—quite an accomplishment!)

When the curtain fell on a *tableau vivant* in which all the protagonists, except my little prince who'd forgotten, froze in place, one arm raised, fortified with a glass of wine, crucified by lighting that was—get ready for it—blue and green; some feeble applause rose from the orchestra seats and the lady who smelled of violets exclaimed, loud enough to pull me out of my lethargy:

"There's nothing as beautiful as a beautiful opera!"

Her husband woke up, grumbling.

"If you like that kind of thing!"

"Hush! You weren't even listening! Wilfrid Pelletier could probably hear you snoring!"

"He couldn't hear me, they were singing too loud!"

The house lights stayed down, only those in the orchestra pit shone softly in the darkness of Her Majesty's, now plunged into the kind of silent daze exuded by a production that's a total failure.

So the conservatory students and other opera buffs had been more perceptive than me. I wanted too much for it to be good, I'd been blinded by my own desire while they showed their disappointment by means of an eloquent silence.

There wouldn't be an intermission between the first and second acts. Which was fine with me, I'd get to see my little prince sooner! We were promised Juliet's garden for the next tableau; the famous balcony scene was coming up. Who knows, maybe Romeo would be accompanied by my bewigged and dusky individual, his best friend and confidant who would be there for the whole scene solely for the pleasure of my eyes. I wished I had someone to look at, because Pierrette and Richard wouldn't be the most voluptuous or most sensual of couples.

Then all at once I realized how mediocre the music that I'd heard in the first act was. I'd been so busy hating the production that I'd forgotten to really listen. Aside from Juliet's "Je veux vivre" already mentioned, nothing had held my attention: the music had been consistently banal—the choruses as much as the arias or ensembles— and sometimes downright lousy. And I hadn't identified with anyone, not one character held my attention—which surely wouldn't have been the case if I were listening to this opera at home. Was it really because the work didn't interest me, or was it because I was in this theatre, in someone else's lack of imagination, some colour-blind lunatic who could see nothing but blue and green, whereas at home I would have imagined a performance to my liking, with my own sense of theatre and my personal palette? After all, I'd often seen plays that I'd read and I'd adored them. So it was the fault of a bunch of incompetents that I felt robbed of the pleasure that my three-dollars-and-a-half I'd spent should have bought me.

Then Wilfrid Pelletier coughed into his fist as if to wake up the general staff numbed by their hypnotically banal production, and on stage we now saw—we should have been ready for it—Verona in *blue and green.*

I could have screamed: it was the set from the first act with one panel shifted to reveal a gallery adjoined by a broad staircase that fat Richard Cassily wouldn't have trouble climbing! No ladder for this porky Romeo, it would be too dangerous—for him and for the audience's sense of the ridiculous. Now, after being robbed I felt I'd been conned! I would have liked the set to turn, the night to be studded with stars, something grand to happen before our eyes, to prepare us for the love duet, but instead here we were in the same environment but with one wall knocked down.

And those same two damn colours that were starting to make me feel really queasy, with the kind of nausea that's slow to come on and that lasts for ages ...

Of my own personal Romeo not a sign, needless to say!

Richard Cassily, who'd had the gall to take off his doublet to force us to look at him in an open shirt over a generous paunch surmounted by two round, heavy breasts that lacked any capillary system—even faint, even blond—pacing up and down while the chorus—which meant that my singer was in the wings—mumbled that the "dark, mysterious Romeo does not hear us!" Then he turned towards us as if this were a concert performance and shrieked his: "Ah! Lève-toi soleil! Fais pâlir les étoiles," in a beautifully clear and powerful voice—he'd obviously been saving himself for this great moment—but devoid of any emotion and even more, of any attempt to embody his character. The tenor sang and that was it and to hell with Romeo, his passion, his youth!

When the aria was over (I'd heard my older brother bleating it in his bath hundreds of times without knowing it was from Gounod's horrible *Romeo and Juliet*), the audience woke up a little and gave the American tenor the first ovation of the evening.

Imperial Violets on my right was overcome with joy and shouted: "Encore! Encore!" while her husband tugged at her bracelets to make her shut up.

"Stop! He's not going to sing it again, he's done!"

"He *has to* sing it again! He *has to*! He can't do that to us! It's too beautiful!"

And Richard Cassily had the gall to bow! That simple gesture, so disrespectful of theatrical conventions and unassailable proof of the megalomania of an opera singer who considers that he transcends everything he sings, that he's entitled to step out of character to receive the hysterical tributes of his adoring public, was so insulting and infuriating that I stiffened in my seat as if I were on the verge of an epileptic fit.

I wanted to leave, to tear myself away from this bitter disappointment of an evening that in my dreams had been as grandiose as a religious ceremony yet had proven to be infuriating, but the appearance of Juliet on her balcony—which was too accessible and barely lit—calmed me a little. After all I wasn't going to make a scene in the presence of Pierrette Alarie, who was doing the best she could, poor woman, to save the evening. To sing in Vienna, Paris, Salzburg and end up here, swallowed up in green, in an attempt to play an even modestly presentable Juliet, was an act of bravura I had to respect.

As my mother would have said, I curdled up and waited for the act to end.

The first love duet seemed endless, even though it was relatively brief. Night music bereft of grandeur, poetry of an unusual poverty; Shakespeare must have been cursing the French from his grave! It didn't augur well for the great wedding night duet which, if it was no more successful than what had come before, would definitely do me in!

I caught myself closing my eyes three-quarters of the way through the scene and for a few minutes it wasn't quite so terrible. But why go to the theatre to close your eyes? So I opened them. I saw Romeo where I'd left him, one hand on his heart, the other raised towards his beloved perched on her fake balcony. His body faced us in profile—no butt, a hanging belly—but he managed to move his head when he sang, not so he could watch the conductor but so we could hear him, so his voice would carry all the way to the top balcony.

Of my bewigged one with the black eyebrows, however, not a sign; he had left his friend Romeo at the garden gate and must have gone home to bed, depressed by this ball that was such a spectacular failure and the nightmarish and hopelessly blue and green night. (I imagined him taking off his wig backstage; sweating like a man possessed, then sitting it on the back of a chair to dry because it had been so hot onstage ... With his curly black hair he now had eyes of a blue that would send schoolgirls of every sex into a swoon ... I was close by with my white steed and the two of us were seething with impatience ... Right, there I go again!)

The act ended with the separation of the two lovers. (At last! Now I can get the circulation back in my legs), and anaemic applause from a crowd of zombies who'd been shown how to clap one hand against the other, mechanically, to pretend they were happy.

A zombie myself, I was beginning to share the cold indifference of the audience; I couldn't wait to hear the comments in the lobby ... but what I heard during the intermission made me even angrier.

To hear them talk, the whole thing was a triumph, the music divine, the sets sumptuous, the costumes stunning, the singers perfect—in a word, it was a grand evening that they'd remember for a long time. All that in the two languages—one more present than the other, of course— and with an enthusiasm that had been totally absent during the first act. The women of course had more to say than the men, who took refuge behind polite assent, hands in pockets and cigars between lips.

Then a question came that upset everything I'd thought so far: did the audience for opera go for the sole purpose of getting bored? If they hadn't been bored to death for more than an hour, would they have been less enthusiastic, less happy? I'd decided that all these fine folk *wanted* to be bored, and if anyone had told me that was unfair and a value judgement, not everyone could share my taste, I would have answered, big deal, I was right because what my eyes had seen and my ears had heard from the very beginning was absurd in its mediocrity.

In the distance I spotted the two redheads, Perrette and Maureen, and I decided to move closer to them and try to understand what they had to say about the production. Perrette saw me coming and blushed, probably thinking I was going to cruise him in front of his mother. He hid his embarrassment behind his soft drink. Maureen had taken off her glasses, which were as thick as Coke bottles and must have made her eyes look huge. So once again she couldn't see a thing and was looking around with her magnificent myopic gaze, surely aware of the effect she had on men but not obliged to put up with their appreciative ogling—for the simple reason that she couldn't see them.

A brief embarrassment: I'm standing next to them, I obviously want to speak to Perrette but, damn my shyness, I don't dare, and he stands there, obstinately silent, while his mother complains that it's too hot in the lobby and they ought to go back to their seats.

"Yes, mother, you're right, let's go."

(His accent is really adorable. Have they just moved to Montreal? And where do they come from exactly? That's what I should ask him ...)

But the moment has passed, they're on their way to the orchestra door.

Maureen walks past me and Perrette, very softly but loud enough for me to know that I'm the one he's addressing, whispers:

"Do you hate this show as much as I do?"

Deliverance and relief! I'm not alone!

I have just enough time to whisper a quick "Yes, yes, yes," and they both disappear, under the admiring gaze of the men who are shamelessly eyeing a Maureen O'Hara who is all graceful movements and falsely ingenuous nods of the head. A woman that beautiful can't be unaware of the reactions she provokes, especially in a crowd like this one where the men are bored to death.

I have two reasons then to stay for the second part—the last, I hope—of this disastrous production. Perrette didn't wait for me to approach him and for the second time he's made the first move, and my guy in the wig may perhaps make another appearance—to the great joy of my already overly available heart.

A few hours earlier, my life was totally empty, and now I was chasing two hares at once. I knew the dangers but I told myself that it was better to lose two hares than to cross the field without spotting even one.

*

Imperial Violets hadn't left her seat during the intermission, but I'd seen her husband disappear in the direction of the men's room. I apologized as I walked past her and saw her wrinkle her nose. Ah! To have the courage of the Dadaists and fart in her face!

To show quite clearly that any conversation with her was strictly forbidden, she plunged her muzzle into her program, which she must already know by heart.

I decide to do something to piss her off.

I lean over to her with a connoisseur's smile.

"What a godawful show, isn't it?"

I really thought I had a certain nerve ...

She turned towards me, downright scandalized.

"What?"

"I said it's a godawful show ... I've never seen anything so ugly in my life ... All that blue and green lighting—it makes me sick to my stomach ... "

First she opened her eyes wide, then she was off like a shot.

"Aren't you ashamed of yourself! You ... You ... How dare you say such a thing? It's a masterpiece, you know, and a masterpiece can't be bad. How can you say a thing like that? Such a beautiful show! Such a beautiful performance! Such wonderful singers! You ought to keep your mouth shut!"

A few of my mother's intonations, some words she'd have used as well, and her way of protesting that was totally familiar to me ... I grinned at her, which seemed to shock her even more.

"Instead of criticizing, if you don't like it just leave! Why bother staying? Eh? You're wasting your time! Go on, leave!"

"It isn't unpleasant to hate something like that, you know."

Her eyes filled with tears, big tears which though they were unsettling, their obvious sincerity overwhelmed me. She took a handkerchief from her purse, used it noisily, then patted her eyes.

"Pretentious little creep. Why do you want to spoil my fun like that, will you tell me? Why did you tell me that out of the blue? Just to be mean? Eh? Just to spoil my pleasure?"

She was absolutely right: why did I interfere with her pleasure like that? What business was it of mine? She'd paid for her seat, she was entitled to like what she was watching. I was ashamed of my spiteful behaviour and it was my turn now to take refuge, red-faced, in my program. But somewhere deep down inside me, the hot-headed eighteen-year-old that I was had a hunch that I was right to think what I thought, though I'd been wrong to say so to someone who couldn't understand me, and I told myself that I'd mull it all over when I got home ...

Her husband came back. She didn't say anything about my rudeness, merely let out, loud enough for the whole orchestra to hear, or so it seemed to me:

"Those damn beatniks never wash, do they?"

Heads turned, disapproving looks, shrugs. She'd won— and it served me right.

*

The second part of the show was an even worse torture than the first (that's right, it really was): the scenes with Friar Lawrence, who was very far from Shakespeare, by the way, were excruciatingly slow, while the direction, which was vague at best, left the poor singers stranded in the middle of the set, uncomfortable in their rented wigs and grotesque costumes. Friar Lawrence seemed to have acquired his habit that very morning, it was so stiff and new—besides being prickly where it touched his neck, so that the poor monk had the tic of a nervous gentleman who keeps tugging at the collar of his shirt because he's hot.

The love duet, the real one, the great one, the long one, was, predictably, sung very well by the two stars—but equally poorly acted by a Romeo who didn't seem to have gotten undressed that night to make love to his wife, out of sheer embarrassment over his unsightly physique, and who was unable to prove any affection whatsoever, being too preoccupied with projecting his voice as far and as loud as possible. As for his Juliet, who was obviously exasperated by this ludicrous partner, she merely did what she was supposed to do, without getting too involved.

Finally, they died, after some more even slower, even duller scenes, but oddly enough the Capulets and the Montagues didn't get a chance to make peace, as the opera ended on a third duet between the two dying heroes—another unforgivable insult to Shakespeare.

As the evening was totally ruined, I consoled myself by watching my favourite member of the chorus, who was easy to spot now that I knew his costume—he just had one, needless to say—and his little pageboy's wig.

His face was really beautiful, somewhat square, the jaw prominent but not protruding, the nose significant but not too big, the mouth full and fleshy, and the panic I could see in his eyes whenever he had to attack a note—eyebrows raised a bit, brow furrowed, eyes focussed on the conductor's baton—went straight to my heart. I thought the show's mediocrity was unacceptable, but him I would forgive him for anything ...

I'd decided I had to meet him.

But that was a problem too, because I also wanted very much to get to know Perrette ...

So now I had to figure out a way to meet both Perrette *and* Periwig. If I waited for Perrette in the lobby after the show, I was liable to miss Periwig at the stage door; if I raced to the stage door and tried to run into Periwig, I'd be sure to miss Perrette and Maureen whom I pictured—why not?—rushing to their personal limousine while I stood there on Guy Street with my feet in cold water.

But I had time to draw up the following plan (which tells you how hard I was concentrating during the last hour of

Romeo and Juliet) before the curtain fell on one of the most agonizing theatrical experiences of my entire life: I would leave during the applause, trampling Imperial Violets and her husband if I had to (she went on swooning, maybe a little too ostentatiously now, at whatever was ugliest on stage, while he went on sleeping the sleep of the just), I'd rush into the lobby where I would wait for my Irish pair who would probably walk right past me; one glance would tell me if I could approach Perrette or at least answer the question he'd asked me at the end of the intermission, I ... I ... I'd take his phone number if he wanted to see me again (but his mother wasn't deaf, she'd realize what was going on, but anyway, I had to come up with something ...), then I would rush to the stage door where Periwig could only be thunderstruck with love when he saw me smile— his first admirer, his first fan. We'd go somewhere for a drink, he'd invite me to his place—I couldn't bring him home to meet my mother after all!—and one thing would lead to another, nature being simple and predictable and our need for affection—mine, anyway—being what it was ...

The plan was extremely ridiculous, I knew that, but I was deluding myself because I absolutely had to believe that two avenues were open to me: I couldn't choose between Perrette and Periwig so in my mind I would steer my way from one to the other, dreaming, as usual, about impossible things, instead of trying to come up with a workable plan.

I was a virgin and already polygamous.

When the show was over, though, I didn't have the courage to impede the enthusiasm of the woman next to me, who was shouting at the top of her lungs some absolutely hysterical *bravo-brava-bravi*, and I waited impatiently for the end of the curtain calls—not many, but Pierrette Alarie and Richard Cassily did get ovations— before I slipped into the aisle, craning my neck in search of Perrette and Maureen. As it happened they were just ahead of me, so we were crammed, nearly stuck together in the aisle, which made things a lot easier for me:

"Yes, I hated the show as much as you did!"

(Traitor! Traitor! You're speaking English again *to please a guy*! How far will you go to make somebody pay attention to you!)

He turned towards me and gave me a helpless smile that was so disarming, so apologetic ("My mother's here, I can't talk to you") that I let them move away under the unkind remarks of the spectators I was blocking on their way to the lobby, the cloakroom, the exit—to freedom after three long hours of martyrdom.

Perrette Hallery disappeared, his beautiful red head standing out above the others, with Maureen O'Hara hanging onto his arm.

He didn't turn around to wave goodbye.

Ten-second-long broken heart.

And now for Periwig!

What if he's Anglophone too?

And heterosexual?

*

A shove in my back, two shadows running past me.

"Don't tell me, Georges, that he's going to the stage door too! Wasn't he supposed to hate the show? If he dares to ask Pierrette Alarie for an orthograph it's perfectly simple—I'll call the police."

HE EXISTS, BUT IS HE AVAILABLE?

A fairly small crowd was waiting at the stage door. It took a lot of courage and a lot of selflessness to plant yourself at the end of a dark alley in the hope of extracting a smile or a botched signature from people who are exhausted after a poor performance and obliged to act as if they'd just experienced a triumph.

A damp and lethal cold had descended over Montreal since I'd entered Her Majesty's; the mild spell was over. The slush had frozen all at once into rough, bumpy ice, especially in the shade of the theatre where there was only one little red light burning, like at the door of a brothel.

Everyone was walking cautiously, which made for a comical and dubious tableau: these well-dressed folks—wrapped up to the ears in their priceless fur or elegant gabardine coats—were mincing across the ice, heads down, looking as if they were watching for pennies to buy themselves a hot cup of coffee.

I saw Imperial Violets but not her husband, who'd probably gone to warm up the car—at the same time filling it with the stench of cigar smoke. (I hadn't actually seen him smoke a cigar, but I was sure that he did.) I left a few people between her and me. I didn't feel like being yelled at in front of everybody, especially because our conversation a while ago had left me with a little aftertaste of piercing guilt that bothered me.

The opera lovers—the men in particular, of course—were craning their necks towards the reinforced door while they struck one foot against the other. They were perfectly silent. A small island of penguins lost in the middle of a North American city. You could sense the anticipation, the excitement at the thought of speaking to a star of the Vienna Opera and the Opéra de Paris, of touching her, maybe, but at any rate expressing their boundless admiration for her. I envied them: they were there for Pierrette Alarie, for Richard Cassily, for Fernande Chiocchio—while I was waiting for someone whose name I didn't even know and wasn't even sure I'd recognize without his disguise as a citizen of Renaissance Verona, as revised and corrected by a costume designer devoid of genius.

Whenever the stage door opened, a wind of hope blew over the frozen little crowd. Some dancers or singers came out in groups of five or six, noisy and merry, pushing their way through the rank and file who didn't protest because it was the stars they wanted to see, not the extras.

A few supporting roles, voices haughty and laughter false, stood at the top of the stairs hoping for discreet applause or requests for autographs, but they quickly realized that they weren't the ones the crowd was waiting for and they disappeared, their laughter and talk even louder. Bravado and frustration, twin teats of those doomed to be eternal second fiddle.

And what was I going to do when Periwig emerged? Certainly not throw myself at him under the eyes of Imperial Violets and ask him to sign my program! That would scare him away and any chance I'd had would be lost. (And your chances of what, by the way, you dreamer?) So without thinking, to ward off blows, to not look too ridiculous when my little Veronese prince emerged, I started asking everyone for autographs. Dancers, singers, musicians, extras—nobody escaped. They consented with good grace, laughing at me a little, but I didn't care, even if I was making a fool of myself: holding out my program, I was already somewhere else whenever a performer signed his name, so I wouldn't miss Periwig in case he stepped into the middle of a particularly solid group of Capulets or Montagues. Later, sitting over the remains of a meal too copious for the late hour, they would probably talk about me, wondering who the young fool was who collected the autographs of just about anyone and didn't even look to see what they'd written in his program. Another maniac who would spend his life imagining he was somebody, just because he had the signatures of a few celbrities.

Pierrette Alarie, radiant and kind, created quite a stir when she came out, nearly making me miss my victim. The diva, after the prolonged applause that had greeted her, stood on the bottom step graciously signing programs, patiently answering questions ("No, my husband wasn't there tonight. He was singing in the Berlioz *Romeo and Juliet*, in Boston. Strange coincidence, isn't it?"), and then, when Imperial Violets asked her if her mother, Mama Plouffe, was there, she declared that she was tired, it had been an exhausting evening, and disappeared towards Burnside Street where a car was waiting for her.

The alley emptied quickly.

Imperial Violets also left the premises without a single look at me, not even a contemptuous one. All the same I was relieved that I'd been spared her wrath and escaped the threatened exposure.

Still under the spell, like all the music-lovers present at this brief but affable autographing session, who couldn't decide to go on their way in spite of the devastating cold, I didn't see a tall young man come out and take some cautious little steps towards the street.

Someone, a girl from the chorus he'd been paired with for the funeral scene, opened the door and shouted:

"François, aren't you coming to the All American with us?"

"Not tonight, I can't ... "

It was him! I'd nearly missed him! And he was speaking French!

"... I absolutely have to go to the El ... "

The El?

The girl wrapped her woollen scarf around her shoulders.

"What time are you on?"

"Some time after midnight ... We never know, they don't tell us in advance ... Anyway, since I didn't know when the opera would be over ... "

"Maybe we'll go and watch you ... "

"Okay, see you later ... "

(He sings in a place called the El! I had to get to a place called the El! But what is it? I certainly can't go and ask him!)

Before he turned back towards the street he stared at me for one brief moment, just long enough for the shadow of recognition to pass between us (whew!) and my heart melted into my heels.

He had on a duffle-coat and a sailor's tuque, with an old guitar slung over his shoulder.

He even gratified me with a smile, a gorgeous one, before he lowered his eyes to the icy sidewalk.

"If you're waiting for Madame Alarie, she's left ... "

"No, no, no, ummmm ... " (Jerk, say something, that's what you wanted, that's why you've been standing here freezing your feet, now move!)

"If it's Richard Cassily, he left by the front door with Monsieur Pelletier ... "

"Ah, I see ... "

"If you want to see them I think they were all going to the Ritz to eat ... "

"No, no, no, that's okay ... I got the autograph I wanted ... "

"Madame Alarie?"

"Yes."

"Isn't she fantastic?"

"Oh, yes."

(Add something, make it last, keep him talking, you can do it!)

But nothing came and he turned to leave.

"Well, okay, so long ... "

"Yeah ... So long."

He was almost more handsome than I'd imagined. In any case he didn't seem to be such a knucklehead as he did decked out as Romeo's pal. And he'd talked to me! I watched him move away, inwardly furious. (Catch up with him, idiot, talk to him, at least ask him something about the El, what is it, where is it!) But my feet were caught in the ice and my tongue was paralyzed in my mouth.

Then he disappeared too, in the direction of Burnside Street. No car was waiting for him. I plucked up my courage—I couldn't just let him go like that—and nearly fell flat on my face running on the ice after him.

He lit a cigarette as he was walking towards Sherbrooke Street. All was not lost. Not feeling brave enough yet to really approach him, I decided to follow him to the El. Unless of course he hailed the first taxi that came along. It was reckless, I risked being told to get lost if he realized what I was up to, but something told me that he might equally well feel flattered.

(Besides, I don't look like a killer, he won't start yelling *murder* if he notices me following him ...)

And so I stayed in the shadow of Her Majesty's, freezing in my coat that wasn't quite warm enough for winter, and waited to put some distance between us before I started the chase.

Other performers walked by, laughing, talking about the All American, about spaghetti, garlic bread, red wine, and I realized that I was famished.

A cake was waiting for me at home, or a rice pudding. I saw myself in front of the TV, cozy and warm, a big glass of milk in my hand, weeping for the hundredth time over the death of the heroes of *L'Éternel Retour* (how about that, another *Romeo and Juliet*) or laughing like an idiot over some clowning by Fernandel whom I was so crazy about ... No, really! Already all my plans for rounding off this evening had been turned upside down, I wasn't going to ruin everything for a French movie, a glass of milk and a slice of chocolate cake, no matter how good they were! That would be too easy. And too pathetic.

*

Climbing up the Guy Street hill on glare ice is an adventure I wouldn't wish on anyone. I nearly landed flat on my face three times, I fell twice—the second time, I didn't think I'd be able to get up, the pain was so bad: I'd banged my knee against a ridge of ice. Luckily, I hadn't cut myself. On the steepest part of the hill I hugged the walls of buildings so I wouldn't lose my footing and slide to the bottom while Periwig took advantage of my fall to disappear forever from the oh so narrow confines of my existence.

If my friends could have seen me running after a young man in the middle of the night, on an icy hill, hoping that he'd deign to speak to me, if they could have read my thoughts, seen the plans I was drawing up, seen my dreams, my secret intentions—I already saw myself in a room on Ontario Street, undressing a body for the first time in my life: would they have simply laughed at me, or banished me forever, hiding their eyes in shame?

I was feeling so ridiculous when I limped my way breathlessly to the top of the Guy Street hill, I saw the situation I was in as so bizarre and so hilarious that I was fantasizing now about describing it in detail to my friends the next day, even if it meant losing them forever. I knew I wouldn't be able to keep it to myself for very long. To live something so comical and not be able to tell it—how horrendous!

If I ever get to talk to Periwig, if anything happens between us, I'll make a full confession afterwards, for a laugh, to get rid of it, to relieve myself too, otherwise I might explode.

Of course there was writing, but over time, writing things I dared not show to anyone had become the very denial of the act of writing. The post-coital interlude was too difficult: after the little death and its very temporary relief, the great one, the definitive one, the one lodged at the bottom of the drawer, had become unbearable. Keeping everything to myself had become intolerable and I couldn't take it any more. I already had too many of those manuscripts that no one but me knew about, the third drawer of my desk was bursting with them. I was frustrated because I couldn't share the ones I had, I didn't want to add another one—a funny one on top of it.

But were my friends ready for the truth? Even one they'd been aware of for a long time (I'd always refused to appear on the arm of a girl because that would have been lying—to her, to me, to the others. So take an eighteen-year-old guy who's never been known to have a girlfriend: what do you suppose he is?), an open secret that perhaps they talked about among themselves in veiled terms, like me, too shy to confront it head-on. They'd probably be as relieved as I would. When all's said and done maybe I was the one who wasn't ready.

Meanwhile, I had better things to do: Periwig was standing at a bus stop, smoking a cigarette, at the corner of Sherbrooke and Guy, and I could see the number 24 approaching, skidding on the ice. The big machine was already crossing Saint-Mathieu Street and would reach the stop within the next minute. I didn't dare to run, but I didn't want to miss the bus either.

He saw me cross Guy Street, displayed a smile that I decided was sardonic (a second's awareness: "What am I doing here? I'm making a fool of myself!") and mashed his cigarette with his heel.

"You're heading east?"

"Yes, yes ... "

The bus pulled up. I was so out of breath I had trouble talking. He went on smiling.

"It's really something, eh, climbing the Sherbrooke hill with all that ice?"

"Oh—yeah, sure ... (Go on, go on, keep talking! Say something stupid, say anything at all—but talk!) It's really something ... "

(Is that it? You can't come up with anything better than repeating what he just said? You aren't just a dummy, you're a fathead!)

He let me board first and I was suddenly aware of the ice and snow on my coat and pants which mustn't have looked very sexy. He knew that I'd fallen while running after him!

The bus was nearly empty. I was making my way to the back, to the old maids' seat, to let Periwig know—I was really sick of calling him that, his name was François, from now on that's what I'll call him!—that he could sit wherever he wanted, he wasn't obliged to talk or even sit with me ... Why am I so damn shy? If only I could have forged ahead, let him know quite candidly that I was interested! He walked the length of the bus, plunked his guitar down beside me, collapsed on the seat, and unbuttoned his coat.

"How far are you going?"

"Papineau."

"Ah, okay. I'm getting off at St. Lawrence."

So he sang on the Main? He sang in some hole?

We were driving past the Museum of Fine Arts where I'd only once set foot, because I'd thought the place was so snobbish and elitist. I'd rather do without paintings than be judged by a bunch of ladies who thought I was too poor and not artistic enough to walk the august corridors of their illustrious institution. Paranoia, I know, but I couldn't help it, I was so sure that the Museum patronesses were quite capable of distinguishing between a poor person and a poor artist.

I had the impassion that my seat-mate was trying to find a topic of conversation. My heart was wrung out like a wet towel but of course I sat there mute and motionless.

He made up his mind first, but offhandedly, as if all he wanted to do was kill some time.

"Do you go to the Museum often?"

"Oh, sure, pretty often ... " (Liar! Liar!)

"What do you think of it?"

(Red alert! Red alert! Trick question! Prove you've got a brain in your head at least!)

"Well, see ... I haven't been for a while, but the last time it was pretty interesting ... "

(You haven't proven a thing! What does that mean, *interesting*?)

"I've never set foot in it. Bourgeois painting doesn't interest me."

(Good God! An intellectual! Just what I needed, to meet an intellectual! I should've known: a guy who sings in a place called the El!)

A brief silence, then:

"What did you think of the show?"

(That question I know how to answer! I don't even need time to think.)

"Pretty terrible. Horrible, actually. Pierrette Alarie was good but the rest didn't cut it. The sets, the costumes—it was all pretty miserable ... Mind you the opera's deadly boring for a start ... I hope you aren't shocked ... I mean, you're in it ... "

A great burst of laughter, very sincere and very wonderful, something of a release after a misunderstanding or a frustration.

"You're right! But how do you know I was in it, I could've been in the orchestra, or working backstage ... Besides, I think I went out of my way to be sure that nobody'd see me!"

(He's fishing, go for it!)

"You were wearing a ludicrous piss-yellow wig and a blue cap ... "

As if that was exactly what he'd wanted to hear, he merely smiled and shifted his gaze to the street.

(The bastard! He just wanted to be sure I'd noticed him! That was too much! Why would a good-looking guy like him be interested in me anyway?)

I didn't know if I was white or red, but I did know that I'd suddenly changed colour.

We were nearly at our destination. At his.

He held out his hand.

"My name's François Villeneuve ... "

I couldn't get my own name out; I just held out my own hand.

"If you ever want to hear me ... I sing my own compositions at the El every weekend ... You know where that is, the El?"

"No."

"It's on Clark Street just down from Sherbrooke."

And he was gone before I realized that might have been an invitation.

(Make up your mind! Do you want me or not?)

As soon as the bus started, I jumped to my feet (don't think it over or you won't do it!), raced to the mechanical door and grabbed the bell pull like a desperate man.

We'd see!

(Again! You poor fool, what're you getting mixed up in now?)

Getting off at the next stop, in front of the Collège Mont Saint-Louis, my left knee hurt and my limp was a little worse.

*

I didn't find the El right away: I mean I saw it before I realized that it was my destination. There were two cafés on the west side of Clark Street between Sherbrooke and Ontario, the La Paloma and the El Cortijo, and it wasn't till I'd walked past the latter three times—meaning that three times I went up and down the same hill with my sore knee and my slight limp—that I realized it was where François was singing and that the regulars must call familiarly the El because it was shorter and easier than scraping your throat on the Spanish when you got to the *j*: El Cortijo? El Cortillo? El Corrtihhhhho? Was it one of those bohemian hangouts they'd been talking about in the papers? Was I finally going to meet a genuine Mimi, a genuine Rodolfo, a genuine Marcello? And would they sing? (Shut up, asshole!)

Two cement steps went down to a wooden door with a frosted window that filtered the orange lighting. But no sound, no over-loud music, no buzz of animated conversation came to me. It must be a very peaceful place ...

As soon as I'd pushed open the door, the stench of stale smoke, sweat and overly strong coffee floated above some twenty wooden tables where there were dozens of Juliette Grecos and unripe Jean-Paul Sartres, sporting berets too big for their heads, were conversing over empty coffee cups before a very limited audience who from all appearances weren't even listening.

Real beatniks! The ones I'd seen until then were characters played by Robert Gadouas or Ginette Letondal, they adorned our TV soaps with a slightly disturbing presence, were inevitably given some severe psychological defects or inexplicable behavioural problems, displaying their contempt for everything French-Canadian in a *Français de France* accent more real than the real one, and always ended up making one of our favourite heroes miserable and suicidal. They were the bad guys and we were taught to hate them—or at least to look down on them. The ones before my eyes, though, had nothing like the charm of a Robert Gadouas or a Ginette Letondal, and they had to get up very early—which mustn't happen very often—if they wanted to inflict any suffering on anyone.

A quick look around. François Villeneuve wasn't there. Already backstage getting ready to perform? I was about to open the door and brave the icy Sherbrooke hill again because I suddenly felt so tired and drained, when it occurred to me, naive as I was, that this was the perfect place to show off my marrowbone. These people, these Juliettes and Jean-Pauls, would understand me! I would look as if I belonged, with my tight pants, my black turtle-neck and my stunning handmade pendant. Who knows, maybe they'd even think I was a jewellery-maker. They didn't need to know that I was going to be a printer, I could let them think I was a sculptor in bone ...

On condition, of course, that anybody actually spoke to me.

One last vision, fortunately short-lived, of milk, chocolate cake and TV, then I decided to stay. Candide had gone around the world, I could go around the city!

A small table for two at the back of the room had just been vacated. I slipped in between the Juliettes and Jean-Pauls, saw a few youthful Simone-style turbans who looked more like fortune-tellers than the author of *Memoirs of a Dutiful Daughter*, before I arrived at my refuge—a haven for a neophyte who hopes to be accepted but does not yet dare to impose himself ... Maybe someone would notice my pendant, ask if it was a lucky charm, if I'd made it myself ... I took off my coat and sat three-quarters on my chair so people could see that I wasn't just anyone. If clothes don't make the man they do help remind others whom they're dealing with ...

My table was under an abstract painting in which magentas, yellows, fuchsias and reds predominated. The effect was busy but very beautiful. At home I'd never dare to say I liked it for fear of being jeered at to death—my father and brother would have heaped insults on the lazy painter who just splashed paint onto squares of canvas instead of getting a job like everybody else; as for my mother, she would have burst out laughing, saying somebody must have let a child play with paint for too long without supervision—but here, in this far too fragrant setting where I already sensed an open-mindedness that was new to me, I could afford to let myself be stirred by the clash of bright colours that was still imprinted on your retina after you'd stopped looking at the painting. Approaching it—I'd got halfway out of my seat to press my nose against the painting—I realized that it was lit from behind, that it had been painted on something that resembled crumpled plastic, and I thought again about my mother who probably would have said that when you get right down to it, it was nothing but an overly fancy lamp. I didn't know enough yet to look for the painter's name and I resumed my pose, fiddling with my marrowbone the way some women do with a string of pearls.

A blonde, anorexic Juliette Greco was already standing at my table. Her hair was so long and straight it must dip into every cup of coffee she served.

"What can I bring you? A coffee?"

Moment of panic. I'd never drunk coffee after six p.m. and even then it was just as a favour to my mother when wanted to empty that morning's coffee pot. In our house coffee was made for the morning.

"We make great espresso ... "

She must have seen the panic in my eyes at the mere word.

"It's your first time here, right?"

Did I detect some disdain in her voice? Even if I had I wasn't going to be impressed by a local Juliette Greco whose hair probably tasted of coffee!

"Does it show?"

Saying the words, I realized it was the wrong question, but she took pity on me.

"Make up your mind, the show's about to start and François hates us to use the coffee machine while he's singing."

"Ah ... is François Villeneuve singing tonight?"

"Why do you think it's so full? Nobody but François and Tex can bring in such a crowd."

I had to pick the idol of Montreal's beatniks!

"I'll have an espresso."

"Double?"

(She's trying to kill me!)

"Okay ... sure ... why not?"

"It's really good and strong, you'll see."

With a sarcastic little smile she pointed to my marrow-bone.

"You didn't have to bring your supper scraps! Especially when most of our clients are vegetarian."

Vegetarians? What did that mean, vegetarians? I finally guessed what it probably was, but I'd never heard of people who only ate vegetables. How did they do it? Where did they get their protein? At school they'd always told us we should eat bacon every morning and red meat every day ... They must all be sick! I checked out a couple more closely. No, no, no, these people weren't healthy ... their bad complexions, their hunched backs ...

So my marrowbone was *persona non grata* here too. Would I have to take it off to make people realize that I existed? If not, would I be attacked the way Imperial Violets had attacked me at Her Majesty's? Were Montreal's beatniks and nouveaux riches bound together by their shared hatred of my marrowbone? It must be true that in the end left and right always meet! (I'd started to check out the periodicals from France in the Municipal Library and some of the theories I read there upset me a lot.)

My coffee arrived quickly.

The blonde Juliette Greco set the little cup in front of me and a whiff of wet armpit (or of sweater underarm in need of washing) pinned me to my chair. It took all my self-control not to wince and pull back.

"That's thirty-five cents."

(Thirty-five cents for a coffee! In a cup the size of a thimble! The coffee I sometimes drink at Woolworth's on Mont-Royal costs one big fat dime!)

"I'd like you to pay right away, Bones, otherwise it won't be till the show's over and I might forget ... Or you might ... "

"Trust rules supreme!"

"I trust my regular customers but I've never seen you before."

"Do I look like a thief?"

"Thieves rarely do."

"If I was going to steal, I think I'd find something better than a double espresso in a tiny little cup."

"There's no small theft for a thief!"

"No, but there's such a thing as goddamn annoying waitresses!"

She gave me with a big grin.

"Get a waiter's job in a place like this, kiddo, and it before long you'll be annoying too! Nothing personal, but I'd like my thirty-five cents ... plus a tip, if possible ... but you don't have to."

"I've got manners ... "

"You're the only one in this place that does."

I had two dollars left. The show absolutely had to finish before the last bus (it was already past midnight) or I'd have to walk home—with my sore knee and my gimpy leg. Then I remembered that the last bus leaves Atwater at twenty after midnight ... If I didn't meet Prince Charming in this place—but the smells were already turning me off—if he didn't own a stunning white steed to transport me to his palace of marble and glass for the purpose of subjecting me to the latest indecencies, I'd be due for a long walk in the ice and a long week in my bed quaking like an aspen under the assaults of a fever that would be lethal at the very least.

I paid, acting as if I weren't counting my money (hoping a fifteen-cent tip was enough), then Juliette of the Armpits walked away, zigzagging through the tables.

I dipped my lips into the hot, black, thick liquid. Warmed-up pipe juice burned my tongue, then it slashed my throat and demolished my oesophagus. My eyes filled with water—I was sure it was the coffee coming back up already—and I had to pretend to cough into my fist so I wouldn't seem like the uncultivated boor I was to the four people at the next table who seemed to be wondering—or maybe it was my paranoia again—why I was choking like that. It was a while before I got my breath back, then I pushed the cup away for good, regretting my thirty-five cents plus tip.

The lights went out—actually, my blonde Juliette had simply flipped the switch next to the cash—and some feeble applause rose up into the air that was thick with smoke. I had a certain sense of déjà-vu and worried that I was about to see a tuxedo-clad Wilfrid Pelletier who wouldn't smell at all.

Heads turned in the direction of what served as a stage—a chair in one corner of the small room—and someone came on who wasn't François Villeneuve.

He got a fairly warm reception and I realized he must be the other star, the one they called Tex. He was tall, with curly blond hair, all mustache and beard, sexy in his way, with the friendliest face I'd seen since I arrived: his smile was broad and sincere, his eyes sparkled mischievously, and he seemed very glad to be there. I was convinced—because of his happy face and his red cheeks—that this man was not a vegetarian.

"Thanks for coming, cretins ... "

(Not quite the same style as Wilfrid Pelletier ...)

"I know you came to hear François Villeneuve, who made his operatic début tonight alongside his fellow-singer Pierrette Alarie (applause, some shouts, some boos) ... but before I make way for François, I'd like to perform a few little things of my own. I know you know them all by heart because I don't see a lot of new faces here tonight ... "

Heads turned in my direction; I stuck my nose back in my coffee, though I'd sworn not to.

"But tough luck, if you want to hear somebody else, go somewhere else, you bunch of no-goods ... "

My father hated guitar-strummers—if Félix Leclerc appeared on TV he automatically broke out in hives, or so he claimed—but I'd learned to adore their songs through the Radio-Canada variety shows, which had been swarming with them for years now, and through Sélect records, which were trying to broadcast their talent right across Quebec. For months I'd been bellowing "Combien coûte l'amour," by Jean-Pierre Ferland, "Au bassin Louise," by Hervé Brousseau, and "L'Oeil en feuille, au milieu de l'eau," by Jean-Paul Filion—this last one I'd discovered on Renée Claude's first record—and my mother couldn't stand him, claiming I was going to make her loathe the songs she thought were wonderful because I sang them so loud and off-key.

After putting his foot on a chair—so Félix has offspring, how about that?—Tex struck up a fairly amusing refrain. The audience reacted in two ways: either they sang along and even louder because they knew the song by heart, or they lost interest altogether in what was happening on the improvised stage and went back to chattering. He seemed used to it and didn't take offence.

Two or three songs later—a mixture of rural roots and urban political-poetic frenzy full of vigour and life—he set down his guitar, his hands on hips, and looked intently at the spectators closest to him.

"You turkeys really don't want to hear me tonight."

Some laughs, some nice retorts, other more acerbic ones when real irritation broke through.

"When you go to the Comédie Canadienne you put up with their supporting acts!"

He'd set a trap for himself; the replies rang out like shots.

"Who goes to the Comédie Canadienne!"

"I saw Jacques Brel sing backup and believe me, that was something else!"

"We'll listen when you sing at the Comédie Canadienne, not before!"

"But we won't hold our breath!"

"Before I shell out five bucks to hear you sing, man ... "

They all seemed to be enjoying themselves, beginning with Tex.

I thought about *La Bohème*, whose second act I'd listened to the day before, about the Momus Café, about Musetta who went to sleazy bars with her old beau to make him pick up the tab for her gang of penniless performers, about the set I'd imagined—very different from this one, with less emphasis on the sense of smell certainly, about the sublime music that erased everything else, especially any woes. Where was the scrofulous Mimi among these fake Juliette Grecos? Was the big guy with the beard at the next table a painter, and did his skinny, nervous friend write sensitive verses for a woman who'd hurt him?

Did I belong here with these modern bohemians fuelled by double espressos? Did I even want to carve out a place for myself? I sensed that François Villeneuve could become the inspiration who'd fill me with happiness and at the same time make me suffer, who both fulfils and plunders, but wouldn't that demand too much energy, reserves of strength that I didn't have. I'd never been sure I was a person who'd experience great things; I sometimes thought that I'd always rather read about them in books, to witness them in movies or listen to them in lyric works unrelated to real life, that while they might move me, they would leave me perfectly intact.

Was love—the real thing—as nourishing as an opera?

To weep over Rodolfo, sure; but to *live* it!

(You'll never know unless you try, idiot!)

Meanwhile, Tex kept up his friendly festival of insults with the crowd.

"Okay, I get it, I'm leaving ... "

Applause, sustained and generous bravos.

"You bunch of ... So, without further delay, as Michelle Tisseyre used to say on 'Music Hall' ... "

"She never said that!"

" ... The person you've all been waiting for, the baritone of the future, heartbreaker of the three sexes—François Villeneuve!"

The guy who came out from behind the counter to stand beside Tex wasn't the one I'd seen on stage at Her Majesty's and bumped into on the Sherbrooke Street bus. What had changed? Physically, nothing: he was still the beanpole with the square face and arms a little too long ... He hadn't altered his hairstyle ... Ah ... the smile! The smile had changed, it was broader, more confident—the conquering smile of a man who feels comfortable and who is sure of pleasing. From the frightened little mouse in blue tights on the streets of Verona, he'd become the rat of Clark Street, the famous professional rat the women talk about, saying: "Watch out for that one, he's dangerous, he's a rat!" someone I'd nearly maimed myself for, a plain old professional rodent.

If I got up right away I might be able to make the last bus—and my chocolate cake—but I'd have to cross the room, disturb spectators, put up with insults for my bad manners and ridicule for my marrowbone ... François would see me for sure, he might even yell at me in front of all these people ... (I was an expert at coming up with snappy remarks too late); maybe he'd even go so far as to denounce me ... I knew I was on a slippery slope but I was so mad at myself that I was ready to let my heart be flayed. Better endure a recital by the baritone of the future ... while hoping of course that he wouldn't give a piss-poor performance.

He was divine.

Ferland, Léveillée, Vigneault, Brousseau, Desrochers, Lévesque and all the others—even the great Félix Leclerc himself would have to watch out, a great *chansonnier* was being born right before my eyes, and he was going to sweep everything in his path if he so desired. After one song—he'd opened with a heart-rending lament by a little boy who was making his first communion in a state of mortal sin—I was glued to my chair; after four, I was madly in love. With him, with his talent and with what he did with it.

Until then I had hidden my sexual orientation by writing abstruse little pieces that no one but me could decipher; he was doing the same thing—you could never be sure he was talking about *that*, you could only suspect—but with a massive talent that left you gasping for breath at the end of every song—and were ready to kill to hear another. I had the impression someone was speaking to me personally for the first time. The other *chansonniers* I admired were resolutely heterosexual, while this was a unique moment, deeply felt. I was struggling, though, telling myself that I mustn't let myself go, that I'd decided he was going to be bad because he might possibly represent a threat, but his talent was more powerful than anything else, his songs went right inside me, demolishing all my defences.

They weren't lyrical flights like Genet's; rather they had the simplicity of Clémence Desrochers and her lovely sincerity, but transposed to another world, a world even closer to me if that was possible (to date, Clémence had been my absolute idol among the Québécois *chansonniers*), of which I could say that it was my world and that he spoke to the smallest, most sensitive fibre of my being.

Just before his second song, François spotted me at my table at the very back. He locked eyes with me as if to say, "We've come a long way from Gounod, haven't we?"

Yes, and there was a good chance that we'd never want to go back!

He didn't take himself for Félix Leclerc either; after singing his first song standing behind his chair, he simply sat down, smiled at the applause, tuned his guitar while talking to the audience—that was when he spotted me— and stayed there, his head barely standing out above the others, his intelligent face floating in the amber light from the tiny spotlight. And he was singing just for me. I knew that everyone else there felt the same way, but I was convinced I was right (as they did too, most likely).

His images passed over me like brief but powerful revelations that I didn't have time to analyze but that fit together like the pieces in a well-chosen anthology of thoughts I'd never tire of dipping into, of that I was sure.

François Villeneuve was however only slightly older than me, I wasn't sure he was even twenty-five, but his songs were those of an artist who's been creating for years and has come close to the summit of his art.

Everything I'd written so far—my fantastic tales, my realistic plays, my rough drafts of opera libretti—seemed so insipid, so pathetic compared with what I was listening to, that I experienced a long and painful moment of jealousy. A white-hot needle had penetrated my heart and was poking around in whatever ugliness it could find. But once that moment had passed, astonishment, admiration, love—yes, I was convinced that it was love, that admiration had to mingle with desire—came back full strength and overwhelmed me for good.

His set was too short, three-quarters of an hour maybe, but he was deaf to the howls and rhythmical applause that begged him to stay on his chair, to put his fingers on the strings of his guitar, to enchant us again—and forever, if possible—with those brief slices of life that had us spellbound.

The lights came back up, the applause died down and the house sank into a revealing silence: the café Jean-Pauls dared not pontificate any more and their disciples no longer felt like pretending to listen to them. The heads of all the Juliette Grecos were turned towards the toilets—the artists' dressing rooms?—where François had disappeared. A few men sitting in the front row, whom I hadn't noticed before, had their eyes glued to the door of the toilet too, which reminded me again how unimportant my presence at El Cortijo was that night. If François already had a fan club of homosexuals—and these seemed particularly enamoured—it would be best for me to withdraw right away—to avoid too much suffering or to be consumed before I'd even had the chance to consummate my desires.

I was so far removed now from the plan I'd spent all week drawing up that it was ridiculous. I'd begin again, some other time.

I was already on my feet with my arm reaching for my coat, which had had time to dry in the surrounding heat—and no doubt to be permanently saturated with the delicious aroma of unfiltered Gitanes—when François emerged from the toilet. We were face to face, I couldn't not say hi. He said hi back, and shouted at me from one end of the café to the other: "Wait, I have to talk to you!"

Fifty people despised me. To my surprise, I was flattered, appreciating their jealousy almost as much as being noticed by François.

I sat down again, rubbing my knee. I'd actually forgotten my pain while he was singing.

He threaded his way through the tables, shaking hands and dismissing compliments with a shrug—the enamoured tried to hold onto him a little longer, became too insistent and soon found themselves in front of a François who was completely closed and pitilessly cold—then joined me after kissing some of the most fervent Juliettes.

"How about another coffee?"

He took my coat, draped it over the back of the chair, sat down.

"No, thanks, I'd be awake all night."

"You're intending to sleep?"

"Ummm ... yes."

It obviously wasn't the reply he'd expected. He drummed on the wooden table with his fingertips.

"Honestly, you astonish me."

Me, astonish him? After the performance he'd just given?

"Why d'you say that?"

"Listen ... Let's be frank ... Did you follow me from Her Majesty's?"

I definitely liked him better on stage than in real life!

"Was I that obvious?"

"No, but I wanted to be sure ... I'd rather you were frank with me than make up some far-fetched reason for being here ... Did you like my songs?"

The question had come with no transition, like a question held back for too long that you blurt out to get it over with. And what came out of my mouth in all its banality was several million light-years from what I really thought.

"Yes, and I sure wasn't the only one! Is it like that every time you sing?"

"That doesn't matter ... Listen, you're the first stranger—sorry to call you that ... you're the first stranger to come and listen to me for a long time ... I'm sick of always singing for the same people who know my songs by heart and aren't objective ... I'd like you to talk to me and tell me what you thought ... You seem pretty bright ... "

He must have seen the disappointment on my face because all at once he went red.

"I didn't put that very well—let's go somewhere else and talk."

"Somewhere else? Where?"

"I was thinking about going to the Quatre Coins du Monde before it closes ... "

My plan!

"It's too late and ... "

"Your mommy's waiting up?"

"No, it's not that ... but I haven't even got two bucks on me ... "

"Never mind, I got paid, it's on me. I've even got enough for a taxi ... "

"Fine, but I won't have enough to get home afterwards ... "

"We'll see about that when the time comes ... I'll lend you some ... if I've got any left ... if not, we'll work something out ... "

He had a good laugh at my embarrassment.

"You aren't used to acting on a whim, right?"

"I'm not used to being bossed around!"

"Sorry ... I don't want to do that ... Look, I understand, if you come back some day we'll talk about it then ... "

I didn't have time to reply—to tell him to fuck off, actually—when there was a big racket at the door. A woman came in, very upset, her coat undone despite the cold, her voice haughty and dramatic.

"Somebody stole Gilles's songs!"

She spotted François and rushed over like a runaway locomotive.

"François, somebody stole Gilles's songs!"

She looked me up and down.

"Who's this?"

I stood up, introduced myself.

"Delighted to meet you. Françoise Berd."

Her name sounded familiar; she looked familiar too, but I couldn't place her.

She went on without giving François time to open his mouth.

"Imagine, we were coming to hear you sing after we'd visited a place across the street ... I told you, didn't I, there's a place for rent on the other side of Clark Street that I may take to reopen l'Égrégore? Yes, I did tell you, I remember ... Anyway, I told Gilles, let's meet around eleven-thirty, I'll show you the place and then we'll go and hear my darling François, you'll see, you'll be blown away, you'll want to help him out ... Anyway ... He turns up, he looks at the spot, tells me I should rent it, Roland was with us, André too, and when we leave ... Listen, somebody stole his car and everything in it! His briefcase with the manuscripts for his new songs, everything!"

The whole café was drinking in her words. She turned towards Tex who was on his way to our table.

"Somebody just stole Gilles Vigneault's new songs!"

The sudden declaration of World War Three wouldn't have had more of an effect. It was as if a bronze weight had dropped from the ceiling and frozen El Cortijo forever in a *tableau vivant* representing Tragedy Visiting the Beatniks. François broke the silence by putting his hand on the shoulder of the messenger of doom.

"Where's Gilles now?"

"On his way to the police station. With Roland and André. Oh, God, what if he can't find them? Can you imagine that, losing songs?"

And François made one of those unfortunate replies that are so revealing and that you wish you could take back the minute you've said it, when it's inevitably too late.

"Big deal, he'll write some more!"

So much for the esteem and respect of the fifty people there. Everyone liked him a lot, must have seen him as representing the new generation the papers were already clamouring for as soon as the first generation of post-Félix singer-songwriters was born, a good many found him to their liking and would have moved mountains to have sex with him, but until further notice, Gilles Vigneault was *sacred* and even he couldn't touch him without getting his fingers burnt.

He tried right away to make a joke of it, but no one was fooled.

"Hey, come on, he's not senile, he must remember some of them, it wouldn't be that hard to piece something together ... "

No one said a word; some hung their heads.

They looked as if they were making an act of contrition in his place. As for me, I felt more like laughing at such silly devotion.

So instead of making honourable amends or concocting some apology that would satisfy everyone, François blew up.

"Why the long faces? A song's a song, for chrissake, it's not the manuscript of the *Rite of Spring* that's gone missing! Put things in perspective! I can guarantee you're all taking it harder than he is! I bet he'd be the first one to laugh about it—and then get down to work!"

He was getting in deeper and he knew it. He fell silent.

Françoise Berd took him by the arm and tried to lead him to the door.

"Come on, I'll show you the place while we wait for him to get back from the police station."

"I'll just pick up my things."

Looking dejected, he glanced quickly in my direction.

"Are you going to wait?"

Did I have any choice?

I did actually, but the prospect of going to see a place that might become a theatre, of meeting some performers in person, of being introduced to the great Gilles Vigneault himself, overcame my hesitation, reduced it to a very simple warning of danger, in fact—(You'll be even more lonely and unhappy when you go to bed tonight!)—which I just ignored and brushed aside.

"Yes, come along ... We'll wait for you outside."

Françoise Berd had taken me by the arm.

"Have you known François very long?"

"No, not at all really. I saw him in *Romeo and Juliet* tonight, we talked afterwards ... "

"That's right! He had a walk-on tonight! With everything that's happened I forgot to ask how it went. Could you see him at least?"

"With a blond wig and a little blue cap he was hard to miss."

Her laughter was both gentle and booming, like nothing I'd ever heard; it was both thunder and running water, it made you want to be with her and to hell with everyone else. She wiped her eyes.

"My Lord, here I am laughing while poor Gilles is trying to explain to the police that he doesn't care about the car but they *must* find his manuscripts!"

François came back, guitar slung over his shoulder. The goodnights people granted him were tinged with rebuke and no Juliette Greco gave him a hug. My jealousy was no longer a problem, now I could breathe.

*

Outside, it was even colder than when I arrived, the ice as sharp as a field of razor blades. I was extra careful crossing the street, with François and Madame Berd holding me up. She looked at me contritely as she asked:

"Forgive me asking but do you always limp like that?"

François snickered.

"No, he hurt his leg chasing after me ... "

I freed myself and folded my arms right in the middle of Clark Street, like a sullen child.

"Hey, take it easy!"

François took my arm. Did his devastating smile come automatically, whenever he needed it? Or did he not even have to think about it because it burst into bloom all on its own? And the worst thing was, it must have worked every time because I felt myself go limp to the roots of my heart and start talking very softly.

"Why'd you say that?"

"You aren't going to deny it!"

"You don't have to say it in front of your friends! And the way you said it, as if I'd been chasing you for months!"

"It was a joke! Look, there was no malice in what I said, I swear."

He seemed sincere. But who knows with that kind of guy.

Françoise Berd had taken a huge padlock key from her purse.

"If you two ever see each other again it won't be a pretty sight! I want you to promise you'll invite me to your hissy-fits."

*

It would take a lot of imagination to see a theatre in that cramped and overheated space, an old factory—which made what? Shirts? Cardboard boxes?—that was about to move into larger premises and whose owner was prepared to rent for not very much. But Madame Berd seemed to have unwavering faith in her dream and she explained it all with much conviction and many details: the stage would be where a huge machine with metallic arms still stood, the rake of the rows of seats (wasn't the ceiling a little low for a raked house?), the dressing rooms—small but, she hoped, comfortable, the lighting system—barely adequate, but enough for such a small house and, most of all, the atmosphere that would reign in this small theatre devoted to modern authors.

She became lyrical, stopped looking at us, seemed not even aware of our presence. I had the impression I was watching someone dream out loud; it was a beautiful sight, a grand one, even and touchingly naive. But then, no, as I listened to her I quickly realized that she was not at all naive: beneath her lyrical varnish, she was all stubborn determination.

"I'm want my own place so badly, you can't imagine! I've produced enough here and there, in other people's spaces, shows that would work better if we were really at home! We're beginning to have an audience, you know, fans of l'Égrégore who want to see shows by l'Égrégore, and I won't let go until people can see a l'Égrégore show *at* l'Égrégore!"

Now I could place her, with her cracked voice and her unshakable enthusiasm. I'd often seen her interviewed on TV and what she had to say was always fascinating. A former assistant engineer at Bell, she had founded a theatre troupe a few years earlier along with some friends, which they financed with the small amount of money they all had. I'd seen their amazing production of Dostoyevsky's *A Gentle Creature,* produced by Roland Laroche, with Marthe Mercure, and I was still moved whenever I thought about it. Eternal vagabonds, they were looking for a place where they could settle down and it seemed that they'd finally found it.

We hadn't been there for ten minutes when she'd already promised and predicted that François would have his first huge success in this very place—even though the theatre hadn't been built yet. François pretended to listen, letting himself be lulled by fine promises, but a glimmer in his eyes, like a drop of water in his irises that moved slightly when he was concentrating, told me he was looking further ahead; if he ever left the El he wouldn't be content with crossing the street to strum his guitar in front of more or less the same audience.

Madame Berd was looking at me like someone very sure of what she's saying, even if everyone around her is doubtful.

"Let me have your address, I'll invite you to our opening. And to the first première of our François!"

Our François?

Was she marrying us?

I'd be happy to lose my virginity with him if he wanted, but I wasn't ready for the house in the suburbs, the dog, and the canary in the cage ... I mean, really!

Footsteps on the stairs, a breathless voice.

"Françoise, did you forget something?"

André Pagé, an actor who made all the girls (and certain boys like me) swoon on a TV show for young viewers, came racing into the factory. He was so handsome that the premises looked less ugly when he got there. François shivered a little, like someone made uncomfortable by a force that he couldn't control.

André Pagé held out his hand

"Ah! Hi, François ... "

After the introductions (I'd again had trouble saying my name because I was so impressed, and I wasn't sure he'd understood it; in fact, I had the impression he wasn't at all interested), he went on, speaking to Madame Berd.

"I thought you'd gone home, I phoned but there was no answer ... "

"Did Gilles find his songs?"

"No, and the cops told him it was very unlikely he ever would."

Since I was expecting the disastrous expression on Françoise Berd's face, I glanced in François' direction. I'd been wrong, there wasn't the faintest glimmer of triumph in his eyes. He wasn't jealous of Gilles Vigneault, he seemed genuinely sorry. He went up a notch in my esteem.

The director of l'Égrégore shook her head.

"That's my fault too. If I hadn't invited him to come and see the theatre ... "

"Françoise, stop blaming yourself, you aren't responsible for anything ... And will you please stop calling this a theatre, it's far from a done deal!"

"Where's Gilles now?"

"He left, what did I tell you ... He told me he'd try to copy them from memory as soon as he could, while they're still fresh in his mind."

François shrugged.

"You see?"

Madame Berd took the key out of her purse again and headed for the stairs.

"Meanwhile, would you like to come to my place for a drink? I'm not brave enough to go to bed right away, I know I wouldn't sleep."

Faint protests from everyone; André Pagé wanted to go to bed, François confessed that he intended to close the Quatre Coins du Monde to dissipate the adrenalin he'd accumulated over the evening's two performances, and I wanted to go home and rest my knee.

"What a boring bunch! The night's still young!"

She took me by the arm. This time it wasn't to help me but to persuade me to follow her.

"My martinis are famous all over town, you know!"

"I've never had one in my life. I've never even had a beer!"

"It's never too late to start! And I'm the obvious one to initiate you!"

André Pagé shook his head, smiling. He had stopped at his car.

"Don't push it, Françoise! If he doesn't want to drink, it's his business. And offering him a martini at this time of night—honestly!"

He turned towards us.

"I can give you all a lift if you want ... "

*

So there we were, the four of us, in his car: Françoise in front, François and me in the back. I had protested (but the singer and Madame Berd hadn't) and André had said it would do him good to drive around town for a while before he went home, it would relax him.

"Where do I go first?"

He was looking at me in the rear view mirror, so I spoke up.

"I live in the east end ... corner of Cartier and Mont-Royal."

François jabbed me with his elbow.

"You said you'd come with me ... "

"I'm wiped out ... Another time ... "

"You aren't going to drop me like this ... "

He leaned forward, rested his chin on the back of the front seat, between the two passengers.

"He's coming with me. How about you two?"

Françoise laughed. She straightened her fake-fur hat which she'd caught on the car door when she was getting in.

"Those places aren't for people like us, François."

"They let in heterosexuals."

" ... But they aren't welcome and I'm not in the mood to be gawked at like a Martian in a fur coat who doesn't know what to do with her feet. And André's too well-known to go there. You know how quickly you people jump to conclusions!"

I patted François's shoulder gently.

"I'd really rather go home ... I'm tired ... "

"A promise is a promise ... "

"I didn't make any promise ... "

"I did though ... I promise on the head of my guitar I'll take you home, no matter what time we leave."

The Quatre Coins du Monde was in fact the place I'd intended to go after *Romeo and Juliet*. So I was practically back to square one.

André Pagé was getting impatient.

"Make up your minds, we're at the corner of Ontario; do I go left or right?"

Françoise had turned around and was looking lovingly at us.

"Turn right. I think François has won again."

I wanted to protest, proclaim my independence, insist that they let me open the door, get out of the car, and wait bravely for the next taxi (even though I wasn't sure I could pay for one), but I also told myself, I couldn't deny it, that I didn't have the slightest wish to go home, that fate had brought me where I'd wanted to go from the beginning and that we mustn't go against fate when it's so powerful. If it was written in the sky or somewhere else that I was supposed to go to the Quatre Coins du Monde, I should allow fate to carry me along, to drift where it wanted me to end up, accept its imponderables as a gift, not a calamity.

All at once I also realized that the other three people in the car took it for granted that I was homosexual and it didn't seem not to matter to them in the least. For François it was normal, but for the other two ... So it was possible for heterosexuals to *know* without changing the way they behaved with me? Was the artistic milieu so full of homosexuals that they were almost the norm? Everything people said and the gossip I stooped to read in *Ici Montréal*—the worst yellow rag in town—was true!

André and Françoise even appeared amused at what seemed determined to get under way between François and me. Were they in the habit of seeing him cruise anything that stood still, to string everyone along for the sole pleasure of seducing? And if I played the game (in spite of my tremendous pride, I was in the mood, even if it was just to find out where it would lead me ...), would I be able to stop in time, to pull out before I got hurt? Would I have the courage to run if I realized that François was becoming truly dangerous? Was danger part of love? Not just the danger of loving, but also the danger of loving the wrong person. I'd never thought about that; to date, my dreams featured Burt and Brando, whose only goal in life was to make me happy (physically in particular, of course). And along had come this François who suited my taste completely but whose intentions I couldn't fully grasp, and who seemed to be already thinking that I was totally devoted to him when in fact I was more in the mood to slap him than to kiss him!

I would have certain things to settle before I fell asleep that night! *If* I slept ... For the first time I tried to undress François mentally, but my mind was too accustomed to memories of *From Here to Eternity* or *A Streetcar Named Desire* and I doubted that a guitar-plucker would have physiques like theirs ... Was he hairy? Covered with hair or hairless? Would he know how to ... How would he manage to ... I caught myself dreaming in visual euphemisms, whereas my nights with Burt and Brando had always been very explicit.

My Prince Charming didn't have a steed, his biceps wouldn't pop through the sleeves of his T-shirt, but he possessed a guitar and a huge talent that was liable to take him far; which wasn't so bad, if you think about it.

François had in fact taken his instrument out of its cardboard case and he was strumming chords and murmuring something incomprehensible. Surely he wasn't going to start playing the inspired artist, unaware of everything around him after he'd practically begged me to follow him!

The St. Catherine Street bars were beginning to empty. Françoise was tapping the glove compartment with her fingertips in time to the music.

"When does that Quatre Coins du Monde of yours close? It's getting late ... "

"When the respectable bars close, the disrespectful ones are always there for us ... "

It was going to be a long night!

Which was fine with me!

*

"We'll get out there, at the corner ... You two still aren't coming with us, cowards?"

No sooner were we out of the car—the door hadn't even closed yet—when I heard Françoise Berd cry out:

"André! Look! It's Gilles' car!"

I didn't know which car she was pointing to amid the noisy fiasco of the evening's end and while I was looking everywhere at once; François seemed content to shrug.

We could hear André Pagé laughing.

"Come off it! How can you say it's Gilles' car? You've only seen it once!"

"I'm telling you, it's his! We've caught our thief!"

"Françoise, you aren't going to make me run after a car I've never seen before just because it looks a bit like Gilles Vigneault's!"

"But he'd be so happy if we caught his thief!"

The door slammed, the wheels glided over the ice, and the car skidded away.

There we were at the corner of St. Catherine and Stanley, with François hugging his guitar while I rubbed my knee, trying not to wince.

"Do you think they're really going to follow that car?"

François gave a mysterious smile.

"Those people are ready for anything ... "

HE'S AVAILABLE;
BUT AM I REALLY INTERESTED?

It was a long narrow space in the semi-basement of an old building on Stanley Street, below St. Catherine. The wall on the left was home to a massive bar in varnished wood surmounted by the inevitable mirror that was more or less concealed by hundreds of bottles of alcohol, while the wall on the right was lined with a series of small tables, packed in too close together to act as the oasis of privacy for which they'd been intended. The music, much too syrupy for my taste, poured out as an accompaniment designed to help people forget themselves, and there was the pervasive smell of stale tobacco and alcohol breath. A few of my favourite things ...

It was too dark to really make out the faces of the men who were moving around in this cramped space; there was just enough light to see that all heads turned towards the door when we stepped inside. Hoping that the perfect man, the Mister Right of sleepless nights, the one with the physique of a Greek god and the intelligence of a genius had finally appeared.

François had warned me that the first seconds would be decisive, that you had to make a good impression right away if you didn't want to end up all alone beside the wall, sitting over a lukewarm beer and waiting for Santa Claus. I had confessed just before we entered the Quatre Coins du Monde, that I'd never set foot in one of these bars, but I didn't have the guts to tell him that I'd come here to *be* with him, not to *cruise* with him, which he didn't seem to realize. But I wasn't prepared for this intimidating, terrifying moment, with dozens of eyes inspecting me from head to toe, judging, weighing, sizing up the goods I represented with insolent directness. In Parc Lafontaine every tree could hide a candidate for either seventh heaven or the third sub-basement, and disappointments, when they occurred, could always seek shelter in the protective shadow of the paths lined with maples and elms. Here though, the prospects were all assembled in the same place, sniffing you like an expectant mob, with insulting coldness.

Even concealed by François' shoulder—I'd let him go in first as he was a lot more handsome than me and had experience—I felt myself being weighed, appraised, and quickly classified as "ordinary," one who didn't warrant any effort. I hadn't expected to trigger an onrush of salivating transfixed suitors, but to see myself spurned in favour of a lukewarm beer or a double scotch was new to me and utterly humiliating.

François' guitar seemed to interest a few men for a few seconds, then all at once our arrival sank into the limbo of trivial events to be immediately forgotten. Even François, so sexy in his studied dishevelment, was rejected by this mob of drunken idiots. What were they waiting for? For Burt and Brando themselves to show up here and scratch them where they itched? Or was François a regular who was part of the furniture, whom they'd all had sex with, who no longer interested them because he was stale ...

Still smiling, François whispered:

"It won't be easy, tonight's the night for the tight-assed crowd. We should've dressed up as office workers or salesmen at Dupuis Frères, we'd have had more luck."

Gentlemen in white shirts and respectable neckties, hair combed with Wave Set and as hard as a Varathaned floor, were manoeuvring around the bar, brushing elbows accidentally on purpose; but you could sense a certain urgency in their overly calculated movements and the dejected looks on their faces.

We walked the length of the bar, clearing a path with our forearms and a series of "Sorry"s and "Excuse me"s that everyone ignored. Sighing, François put down his guitar.

"Wasted effort. We might as well leave right now ... There's no room for bums like us ... Besides, those girls are on the verge of hysteria because last call's coming and it's not a pretty sight."

He explained what "last call" was and I was horrified. François was smiling a nasty smile.

"It's no fun to live through, but it's worth watching if you aren't involved. It's fifteen minutes of pure frustration and it's very interesting to see. The most hopeless human beings come to the surface and for a couple of minutes you get a glimpse of the bottom of the barrel. It won't be long, just a few minutes. Want a beer?"

"I already told you, I don't drink beer ... "

"Well you will tonight ... Look, you have to be slightly pissed to watch it or you'll be depressed for the rest of your life. And never want to come back!"

"It's true, I didn't come here to get depressed ... Okay, I'll try one ... "

(Tell him! Tell him! So at least he'll be clued-in, so he won't pass out if you take his hand between sips of beer! Maybe he really doesn't know that you like him! Or maybe it's exactly what he expects! No ... if that's what he was expecting he'd have already invited me to his place, his pad, his lair ... Quit dreaming, you've already stopped listening to what he's trying to tell you.)

The beer arrived very quickly and François—either clueless or cynical—toasted our love lives. The first sip rolled around in my mouth for a while—it tasted like cereal that's been sitting on the kitchen counter for seven years—the second one wasn't quite as disgusting. And starting with the third, I drank mechanically, not worrying whether I liked it or not. And the effect—probably because

I was so tired and so much on edge—was immediate. Bubbles of giddiness went to my head and I lost my balance during the fraction of a second when they burst. It was not unpleasant. Quite the contrary. I was afraid I'd lose control of my movements and my thoughts. I slowed down, taking very small sips, a little like my grandmother's canary when I was a child ... (She'd say to me: "Look at him taking a sip, he drinks nearly as fast as the men in this family!" She would be laughing but I sensed a warning in her eyes. Don't drink. Or not very much. In any case, be careful. And here I was, fifteen years later, trying my first dangerous sip—beer being the absolute and definitive scourge of my family I'd always avoided it at all costs—in the bottom of a well-maintained but suspect cage where at any moment now, I'd witness the cataclysm promised by the guy I'd thought was Prince Charming, but who was turning into just a drinking buddy. Had the men in my family started like this—a beer just to keep someone company, to please a friend, to be like everyone else, to be *a man*? Did I feel more like a man swallowing this extract of fermented hops and barley? More than when I was listening to the third act of *La Bohème*? Did it matter whether I felt like a man or not? Everything was spinning around me a little too fast and I felt a burst of emotion that nearly made me cry.)

François was looking everywhere at once, on the lookout, or so I assumed, for a glance of recognition, a movement of a head, an inviting smile. I, the unlucky imbecile, was watching to see that on his face, but he'd already forgotten my existence, excited by the two beers he'd downed in less than five minutes, maybe unconsciously worried too about the last call that was taking a long time coming. Was he going to leave me there for anybody or anything at all, for better than nothing—just so he wouldn't have to spend the rest of the night alone? And what about me? Wasn't I even as good as better than nothing? I was offering him my virginity—certified and preserved for a moment like this—and he was rejecting it like some worthless and insipid commodity!

I was about to ask him outright—I was finishing my beer and a certain self-confidence was inching up my backbone—when what had been promised was realized.

With sadistic pleasure the bartender picked up a grade-school bell and started frantically waving it, crying: "Last call! Last call! Fifteen minutes to find the love of your life!" Then he turned on a few lights (François had told me that the lighting would get brighter and brighter until the whole bar was lit and the rejects totally confused), adding, though not so loud: "Don't look at me though, I'm too wrecked for cruising tonight! I'm going to skip this round!"

And he was right. Serving drinks for hours in this contaminated air to noisy, anxious strangers thinking about nothing but getting laid by someone beyond their reach and knocking back shot after shot to desensitize himself, had given him a greenish complexion and bags under his eyes that automatically eliminated him from the race, a victim of this cruel Mass even though he was one of the officiants.

François turned towards me. His eyes were slightly glazed and there was undeniable excitement in his voice.

"Here it comes. Take a good look, it's starting ... "

It was true. As soon as the bell had rung, something in the atmosphere of this smoky bar had changed. Everyone had moved at the same time, but not in the same way. Some had clearly been startled and were now beginning to look around while others, more subtle or too smashed, were content to look up from their glasses menacingly. All, without exception, had moved as if they'd been given the starting signal for some demanding choreography.

Bodies brushed against me, faces made miserable by the fear of being alone slid past me, trying to read on my face the shadow of consent; a hand ran over my ass and I closed my eyes because it was not unpleasant and I didn't want to see who it belonged to—someone totally uninteresting or a downright disgusting stranger. I felt a powerful urge to cry because the hand was insistent and I didn't want it to go away.

It was too hot. I'd kept my coat on. I didn't want to hear one more remark about my marrowbone and even less did I want to take it off. So I put up with the dampness on my shoulders, the rivulet of sweat down my back, the rather suspect smell that seemed a product of all that. In fact, it must have been the odour of a hundred men whose testosterone was suddenly being solicited, but I preferred to think it came from me, it was better at turning me into a pitiful case in my own eyes. I was sure that if I got undressed in front of anyone that night, my smell would be so terrible that he'd run away and spread the word all over town; but I couldn't give up on my plan, the humiliation of going home empty-handed and still a virgin would be just too bitter.

François was no longer beside me. I'd seen him drift into the increasingly dense crowd, after whispering: "Wait for me ... I'll be back."

(Fuck you, pal! Stick your guitar up the ass of anybody you want, I'm not interested! You make me puke! Why drag me here just to show me that? And then abandon me just when an unknown hand is trying to convince me that it could bring me a consolation I don't need yet! Because I don't have to be in this place! I'm not so desperate that I have to come here and hide out! You're the one who wanted it! All the way! With your beautiful songs and your beautiful smile! Just fuck off, it's too late, I'm out of here!)

The hand had moved up my coat and inside my pants—from outside, it must have looked completely grotesque—

a finger was trying to worm its way between fabric and skin; I gave my assailant a violent shove—yes, it was an assault, I hadn't asked for this!—and I heard an effeminate voice yelp in my ear:

"My God, you sure are direct!"

As I opened my eyes, I glimpsed salvation just behind the head of a pudgy blond looking at me through eyes bloodshot and swollen from a night of still undigested alcohol. Or so it seemed.

Leaning on the bar, shoulders hunched, nose in a glass of beer with brimming head, red hair glowing like a lantern in the light that had just been turned up a notch, Perrette Hallery was also experiencing the assault of an anonymous hand. Victory! Someone to talk to!

But François Villeneuve was going towards him.

In fact, he was lumbering in his direction through a mass of bodies, and there was no indication that he was actually heading for Perrette, planning to approach him, seduce him, take him away, but in just a few seconds a grand three-act melodrama was unfolding in my mind and I sincerely believed that my life was ruined forever: I was losing my two prospects simultaneously. Snickering, they were on the way to the door, then turned my way to bid me an insulting final farewell as they went off to take a sumptuous room at the Ritz, the most beautiful, most expensive, that never in my life would I be able to afford. Their lovemaking was a toast to my health, in a bed worthy of the Thousand and One Nights (brocade, satin, taffeta, more silk than you could imagine, we're rich, we're tacky, it doesn't matter!), as they laughed at my unhappiness, while I, in a grand sacrificial gesture, vowed to practise total, irreversible abstinence and devote myself to lepers in Africa. It was brief and violent and it did me no good at all.

I had to stop them from seeing each other! A twofold jealousy was spurring me on; neither one of them had the right to prefer the other to me, that was too unfair; I'd worked too hard, hoped too much all evening and it mustn't end like that!

(The two hares! I knew it!)

But which one did I want? And did I really want one? Or did I feel—once again—like going home, hiding under the covers, burying myself away for the rest of the weekend with a sci-fi novel, a stack of newspapers, a whole chocolate cake, and a quart of milk? My virginity could wait one more week, *I had a whole lifetime to lose it!* No, my pride would not let me accept what was liable to happen if François and my Irishman should meet ...

To turn François' attention away from the bar where Perrette had just raised his head to glance in the mirror, I called to him as loudly as I could.

Several heads turned in my direction (either they were all called François, or I'd really shouted) and the singer frowned like someone who's just been disturbed at a particularly important moment. Perrette, also attracted by my cry, had spotted me.

Which one should I speak to? François, to let him know that I wanted to leave, or Perrette, who seemed—was it possible?—overjoyed to see me and was already lifting his glass to my health?

I stood rooted there, with something on my lips that could be taken for a smile to each of them, between a "Let's go now" and "What are *you* doing here?"—at least I hoped so. And to my surprise my attempted diversion was more successful than I could have hoped: not only had François stopped looking in the opera-fan's direction, he had noticed someone he knew and was going towards him all smiles, holding his guitar at arms' length, as if he'd just won a boxing championship. No jealousy this time. He could talk to whomever he wanted, it made no difference to me—as long as it wasn't Perrette.

Who was coming towards me now, his smile even broader, looking genuinely pleased. Was I the consolation prize for him that he was for me? Was I about to be satisfied yet again with a goddamn better-than-nothing?

He put his hand on my shoulder; for a quarter of a second I was afraid he'd take it away because my coat was wet, but it stayed there, curving comfortably around the fabric, pressing down deliberately or so it seemed.

My heart leaped, something in the region of my solar plexus stirred, and for the first time I was glad I had my coat on.

"Hi! What are you doing here?"

(I was in the neighbourhood and somebody pushed me in, idiot!)

I was too exhausted and my pride had been badly mauled that evening, I didn't feel like speaking English, so I answered him in French.

"I came for a beer before bedtime, like everybody else ... "

To my amazement he replied in my language, with an accent so adorable, so sexy (or was it me who was ready to find everything about him exciting under the circumstances?) that I couldn't conceal my surprise.

"Moâ aussi."

"You speak French!"

"Oui. Poorquoi tu dis ça?"

"I don't know why I said it ... I thought you only spoke English. We've always talked English till now ... "

"Si tyu m'avais pârlé français, j't'ôrais répondyu en français ... "

He was right, it was my fault. I'd been too quick to jump to conclusions, I'd assumed he was a squarehead—when it was me whose head was screwed on crooked.

I apologized to him with a pleasure that surprised me, a pleasure that was neither nasty nor masochistic, but the simple pleasure of someone who's sure that he's doing the right thing because he realizes that he had been wrong.

"You don't have to apologize, it's true we didn't speak your language very much ... "

His accent drove me wild and I hid my confusion in my empty beer glass.

"Want another?"

"No, no thanks, I don't like beer ... I didn't know what to drink, I wanted to be like everybody else ... "

Brief attack of embarrassment.

Okay, now what do I talk about to keep him here? He didn't look as if he wanted to run, but if our conversation dropped off too fast ...

The light went up another notch. A horrors! The drinkers around us were starting to lower their heads, to sheild their eyes with their hands; it was really too bright, you could see everything—the bags under eyes, the drinker's noses, the wrinkles of fatigue and frustration. I recognized a few faces I'd spotted at Her Majesty's earlier and I was hoping that all homosexual opera-fans wouldn't end up like that.

Were they all composing their own *Romeo and Juliet* to forget what they were now enduring?

The bar emptied quickly and now there were just a dozen of us—including François, whom I spotted from the corner of my eye deep in conversation with an amazingly beautiful guy disguised as a local James Dean, but who was nearly a dwarf, which made him look disconcertingly like a male doll. They seemed to know one another and to find hilarious what was going on around them. But weren't they part of it too?

Perrette held out his hand.

"I'm Alan. You?"

This time my name came out loud and clear; I was gaining self-confidence and I was really proud!

Alan smiled and went on immediately:

"We have to leave before they kick us out ... It's better for our reputation ... "

He was right—but what to say in reply? To bring up the question that may have been nagging at both of us, to let it be known that we couldn't go to my place but that if it were possible to go to his ...

Did I want to go to his place?

(Make up your mind! This time it might be working!)

"Right, we'd better go ... "

(That's no answer! He'll think you're a moron! Which you are, but he doesn't have to find out right away!)

François and his dwarf were coming towards us now. I would have liked to race away, dragging Alan behind me: I still didn't want my two crushes of the evening to meet.

The introductions made—the dwarf's name was Carmen, he was a painter, and I immediately pictured him painting cancan dancers and posters for the Moulin Rouge—François said we're going to the Tropical, to meet La Monroe, a friend of Carmen's, and one of the funniest guys in town.

"The Tropical stays open after hours and I don't feel like going home right away ... Apparently they've worked up a little show for the regulars ... Carmen can get us in, but we have to hurry because they pretend to close up to avoid any trouble with the cops."

Was he looking at Alan a little too insistently as he said that? And wasn't the invitation directed more at him than at me for that matter? Or was my newly minted jealousy working overtime? Why had he dragged me along at all if the idea was to make me fall for a dwarf painter who spoke with a probably fake Spanish accent? To test his influence on me? Was he one of those people who can't stand it if someone resists and who lose interest as soon as he gives in to their desires? Even more important: were all the artists I admired as different in real life as in their art? François Villeneuve was not at all like his songs, I think that was what upset me most. I'd thought I had found in him the same sensitivity that was in his music, just as I sincerely believed that Jean-Pierre Ferland was unhappy when he sang about being unhappy, that Claude Léveillée had a brother called Frédéric, that Clémence Desrochers had suffered at the hands of sadistic nuns, that Jacques Brel was wallowing in the bleakest misery, and that Léo Ferré lived honestly and fully the anarchy he sang about so well. Was I wrong in the grand naïveté of my eighteen years? When you get right down to it weren't they just a bunch of François Villeneuves who'd been successful, and weren't they living the lives of spoiled brats you wouldn't hear on their records? And what would François turn into, what kind of unbearable monster, once he'd achieved real success? Would he use the people around him the way he was doing that night with me, to achieve his goals, while he laughed at everyone else, thinking only about himself?

Silence had fallen among the four of us. All the lights in the bar were on now, no illusions were possible between anyone that night, and the last late arrivals were either too drunk to leave or too ugly to hang onto their dreams.

The other three were looking at me. They seemed to be waiting for an answer.

"Sorry, I was daydreaming ... "

"Do you want to or not?"

There was no impatience in this question from François, he only wanted to know if I wanted to go to the Tropical. Plucking up my courage, I put as much innuendo as possible into my eyes to ask Alan:

"What do you feel like?"

A great many things happened in the brief seconds Alan took to think it over before he replied: first of all, the fake Carmen gave François a nudge that landed not much higher than his knee, meaning something like, I hope he'll say yes, I think he's cute, then François himself turned his appreciative eyes to me, apparently delighted at my good luck; and the bartender waved the goddamn school bell one last time, shrieking:

"Anybody that's not a couple, quit dreaming, it isn't going to change in two hours, so do like me and go to bed!"

My freckle-face finally spoke.

"Why not ... It might be interesting ... "

Of course I would have preferred (for the third or fourth time that evening) that Alan say no and that he'd then carry me away to his château in Outremont or Westmount, but my fantasies were starting to take a serious beating and I wasn't too disappointed by his reply.

Except that I still didn't have a cent.

Not even for a beer (or a Coke) at the Tropical.

So I intended to leave them at the corner of St. Catherine and Stanley and try to hitch a ride home. My left knee couldn't walk all the way to Plateau Mont-Royal, so like Blanche Dubois in *Streetcar Named Desire* I'd have to rely on the kindness of strangers. But it also meant that I'd be leaving Alan and François alone with the fake Carmen and the plan to go to the Tropical ... Acute discouragement mixed with physical fatigue was making me stagger into the even worse and damper cold of Stanley Street.

François must've been reading my mind because he took my arm and while we were walking towards St. Catherine Street, he said:

"Here's ten, you can pay me back ... "

It was an enormous amount, more than twice what I'd spent to see *Romeo and Juliet*.

"Why are you doing this ... We might never see each other again!"

"Something tells me that won't be the case ... Without your marrowbone you'd look as if you stepped right out of the El. You'll start liking it, we'll see each other, I haven't got the slightest worry ... You'll pay me back when you can. And good luck with Alan ... "

This was the first time I'd met someone I really couldn't understand. He was like a streak of mercury, at once elusive and heavy, sometimes very present at what was going on, then suddenly absent, impossible to follow or, even more, to understand. He was putting me in a difficult situation strictly for pleasure, or so I was convinced—he must realize that I liked him!—and then coming to my rescue with a generosity that was to say the least surprising. *But what was he getting at?* Did he feel some affection for me like a little pet animal you feel just a bit sorry for then console with baby talk, in an outward show of generosity? There were too many questions for one evening, I was beginning to think I should have stayed home, listening to the third act of *La Bohème* with Victoria de Los Angeles or to Callas in the second act of *Tosca*.

Daydreaming was less nightmarish than life because you could control it—that, I'd always known. But I hadn't had a chance to verify it yet ...

I pocketed the money.

"Thanks, but I think I'll use it to get home. I'm tired and my knee hurts ... "

"No way, I'm lending you that money so you can come with us, not go to bed!"

"You're lending me the money period. I can do what I want with it, it isn't yours any more."

Alan and Carmen were a few steps behind us and I didn't dare imagine what they must look like—one so long, the other so short. Did the former Perrette think that

François and I were a couple, that he was catching us in a lovers' quarrel? Was he being sordidly cruised by the poor man's Borduas? Was he simply going to drop us at the next corner and go home, furious at wasting his time with me? I was more and more exhausted and leaving everyone there on the icy sidewalk like a pile of dirty laundry you don't have the courage to wash seemed to me the only conceivable solution.

"It's the first time you've decided to go out, eh? You haven't been around our crowd before?"

I certainly wasn't going to leave him with the illusion that he was a great psychologist ...

"That wasn't hard to figure out, I made all the wrong moves!"

François smiled and I realized that he was holding onto my arm. An hour earlier I'd have given everything for a moment like this, condemned my soul, entrusted my body to the flames. But this touch, which was more friendly than intimate, stirred nothing inside me. We were there already! Was it that easy? No, I knew that if I looked at his handsome profile, his artiste's mien calculated to the millimetre, assembled from portraits of Rimbaud or other dashing poets—now I was doubting even the authenticity of his looks—the urge to take him in my arms, for him to take me, would overwhelm me once again and I'd be back where I started, filled with hope yet ensured in advance of a bitter and conclusive defeat.

And if I turned towards Alan, would the same need— *exactly* the same need—come over me, was I already changing course depending on which way the wind was blowing, hoping for anything at all as long as it gave me shivers, pleasure, relief? Was I searching for love as I'd thought, or only for a powerful spasm that would only cost me my virginity, the first in a long line that would last my whole life and never satisfy me?

"I'm not sure you're even old enough ... "

"Old enough for what?"

" ... To go to the bars."

"I'm eighteen."

"So you aren't old enough, you have to be twenty-one."

(And now a new one! Suddenly I'm an outlaw!)

"Don't I look twenty-one?"

"You don't even look sixteen!"

"If that's a compliment, thanks."

"You seem shocked that I'd say that."

"No I'm not ... "

"It's true, I remember, when I was your age I wanted to look older ... You'll see, that will change in a hurry."

"How old are you? All of twenty-two?"

"All of twenty-three and I'd give you all those years—even if it's not saying much—in exchange for yours ... "

"Have you got something to be forgiven for that you'd like to do over?"

"Do over?"

"I mean mend. Have you got something to mend?"

"No, but I've wasted some time that's gone for good now and I'd like to get that back ... "

"You sound like a little old geezer ... "

He squeezed my arm somewhat harder and his voice dropped a tone, as if an extremely important confidence was going to follow.

"I *am* a little old geezer."

But that was all and the moment passed with neither of us taking full advantage of it. A few steps on the ice, a breath or two, but too late. We'd both just missed out on something important, I knew that, but whether from shyness or fatigue we'd let pass an opportunity that we could have grabbed, and silence fell over Stanley Street with a muffled little sound of defeat.

The other two had caught up with us. Alan seemed bored beyond human endurance and I regretted abandoning him (and I'd probably have regretted abandoning François if I'd gone with Alan).

In the general malaise—Carmen was dawdling and looking at the other side of the street, Alan seemed to want to hail a taxi—François locked his gaze firmly with mine.

"You can't finish your first night on the town without going to the Tropical ... "

And the confidence I'd been expecting from him came from me. I was hardly even aware that I was talking, the words came out of my mouth without my searching for them; the sentence was brief, clear and filled with the childlike naïveté that had not yet left me because I hadn't lived yet.

"I didn't want to go to the Tropical, I wanted to fall in love!"

That wasn't true: I'd wanted both. This first half-lie made my chest swell with confusion. I'd been absolutely sincere while I was telling a lie! I could have wept with shame.

I had nearly rested my forehead against his; we must have looked as if we wanted to kiss. (As far as I was concerned, I would have kissed him right then, I would have married him and been happy with him forever after —for ten long seconds!). He had dropped his hand onto my shoulder.

"Don't worry, it happens to all of us. It happens to me every night. And for quite a while now too!"

If I could claim just once in my life that I'd seen my illusions take flight, it would be now. There was a rustling of their wings as they rose into the night-time sky over an icy Montreal and I bade them a silent farewell with my eyes shut.

"What do we do? Are we going or aren't we?"

The little man had an ugly voice on top of everything else.

"I think I'll go home ... "

Alan's wonderful accent was a joy to hear. I of course let myself dream that I'd be listening to it for the rest of my life; I knew how absurd this daydream was, particularly in the situation in which I found myself, but cynicism—that oh so easy way out when you've missed something—imposed itself on its own and I was relieved. At that moment I chose cynicism and mockery as the two poles of my existence, but I didn't really develop them till much later, because they only come with experience.

François grabbed Alan and me by the arm—he'd have had to crouch down to grab Carmen's—and said very loud into the already lighter traffic on St. Catherine Street:

"Nobody's going home; everybody's going to the Tropical."

*

At this hour, St. Catherine Street was completely empty. A few lingering strollers were sliding towards cars parked on the cross streets, others hailed taxis already transporting revellers with nodding heads on their way home after their weekly excesses, sated with alcohol but sexually frustrated if they hadn't connected with anyone.

The cold must have revived my senses because suddenly, with some concern, I realized that here I was, in the middle of the night, in a part of town I didn't know, in the company of three people whose existence I'd been unaware of a few hours earlier.

I, the faithful friend, the eternally anxious one who always feared that his friends would find him boring and abandon him to his fate, the cowards, because he didn't interest them any more—I caught a glimpse of my silhouette in a St. Catherine Street store window, on the arms of two guys I hoped to make love with in turn, following behind a near-dwarf who seemed to be pointing to the road to hell, like a character in a film by Bergman or Fellini—I'd seen *The Seventh Seal* and *Nights of Cabiria*, which had become the two films of my life—while all my friends had been asleep for ages between their uneventful adolescent sheets. I was the one who'd dropped them on a Saturday night—had they gone to the movies? Watched a movie on TV? Played Tired Tits or Queen of Spades? Had they gone out around nine o'clock for some fries at La Poupette on Mont-Royal Street?—and an embryo of guilt wrung my chest which was already crushed by everything that had happened since *Romeo and Juliet*; if I had stayed with them, I'd have experienced an ordinary Saturday night with no conflict or excitement, in the company of my *real* friends; I'd have gone to bed early after laughing moderately, been pissed off moderately, and for hours by now I would have been dreaming the normal dreams of a normal individual to whom nothing has happened and whose soul was at peace.

My soul was not at peace.

Earlier, I had thought about Candide and his chaotic trip around the world; now it was more like Pinocchio blindly following the unscrupulous fox and dog and cat who were going to sell him to a circus-owner where he'd become a puppet—once again, my hesitant film culture, Walt Disney this time. I smiled inwardly at my fright, but all the same I was afraid I'd finish up in a dead-end situation that I couldn't escape: a bar for homosexuals that was officially closed but that stayed open for its regulars with all that that implied. It was hard for me to imagine, but at the same time fascinating and disturbing. It's true that I was attracted by what awaited me on Peel Street in a den of iniquity reputed for its excesses of every sort—sex, alcohol, even drugs! I was also feeling guilty in advance about what I'd find there, that I was liable to enjoy too much and that—who knows?—I might be unable to live without (my sense of melodrama, inherited from my mother, was never far off and wanted nothing better than to manifest itself at any time, in any circumstances).

I also realized, from looking in the various store windows along St. Catherine Street, what a strange quartet we formed—and that Alan was constantly sneaking peeks at me. Which was extremely flattering.

Did he feel for me what I'd felt for François ever since I'd spotted him onstage at Her Majesty's? Was he dreaming about losing his virginity in my arms or—who knew—making me lose mine because the word "virgin" must have been written all over my face? Or—the horror!—was he simply using me to get to François? And—good God, I hadn't even thought of this—had he just recognized him? (I was exhausted, sick and tired of asking myself since the beginning of the evening questions I couldn't answer; but unable to stop myself, I'd become a veritable question mill.) I'd been afraid they knew each other, I'd been afraid of their meeting, and now I was even afraid that Alan had recognized François—which in any case would have been perfectly normal! I wanted to be clear about it in my own mind and I spoke to Alan as if nothing were amiss:

"François was an extra in *Romeo and Juliet* tonight; did you recognize him?"

François, insulted, didn't give Alan time to reply.

"I wasn't an extra, I was really pretending to sing!"

I laughed spitefully and decided to take advantage of his slip of the tongue to shine in Alan's eyes.

"What does that mean, *really* pretending to sing? Were you pretending or weren't you? Were you a singer or an extra?"

"Pretending, but I was more than an extra. The extras didn't rehearse, they were just told what costume to wear, where to go, and what to do, but I had two rehearsals, I'd learned a few scenes with the choirmaster, I mimicked the words, I knew what was going on, who my character was—a friend of Romeo's, maybe even an *intimate* friend if you know what I mean—and why he was singing what he was singing! You couldn't hear them in the house but the real extras often panicked and kept saying, 'What do I do, where do I go?' in at least four languages!"

"Do you at least get paid more?"

François could also be a bitch and he proved it pronto.

"If I wasn't paid more somebody wouldn't have afforded to go to the Tropical tonight!"

I made a weird sound as I swallowed my own bitchiness, as if I were about to choke on my saliva. Alan, who hadn't understood what we'd just said because François and I were talking too fast or because he quite simply hadn't been listening, was content to answer the question I'd asked him.

"Yes, I recognized him. He was very handsome in his Renaissance tights ... "

(You wanted to know, now suffer!)

François didn't even blush, he was probably used to compliments and took them for granted.

Carmen had turned towards us.

"I would've liked to go to that opera but François wouldn't let me watch him ... "

François smiled (again, that smile that made you want to get down on your knees).

"I didn't feel like hearing you make stupid remarks in the middle of the ballroom scene or when I was working my ass off claiming I was sorry about Mercutio's death when what I really wanted to do was laugh my head off! Or while Pierrette Alarie stabbed herself in the breast with the phoney dagger!"

When I saw Alan having a good laugh I realized that it was pointless to fight the stupid jealousy that tormented me whenever François scored a point, and I allowed myself once again to hate them both.

Carmen stretched out his small frame—the fake James Dean wore girls' boots with stiletto heels, he was even smaller than he seemed, so he really was a dwarf!—and declared solemnly as he pointed to a building on Peel Street north of St. Catherine that didn't look like much:

"Gentlemen—pandemonium, the capital of hell!"

*

The staircase was narrow and smelled of the cheapest perfume. Powerfully. Men who smelled good and strong must have waited for hours on these wooden steps polished by the comings and goings of generations of Montrealers who showed up alone in the capital of hell in the hope of leaving it with someone else. Countless hearts swollen with hope had climbed these stairs and a nearly equal number of deflated windbags had come back down them: under the prevailing sugary perfume hung the more suspect aroma of disappointment and rancour.

A doorman was waiting at the top of the stairs. It was the first time I'd seen one and I would have expected something like a brutal hulk, voice broken by alcohol and cigarettes instead of this fair-haired Adonis in a raccoon coat. He greeted Carmen with the cries of joy of a stuck pig and a not very natural-sounding lisp.

During their outpourings, which seemed to want to go on till morning and even until high mass at ten, François, Alan and I stayed behind, the singer rolling his eyes impatiently, the redhead and I regarding each other with the slightly panicky look of neophytes who don't yet know what they've embarked on and would run away if it wasn't too late.

Carmen introduced Manon—clearly, opera was dogging my every step!—and he, or she, in any case the individual gave Alan and me a surprisingly firm handshake, job *oblige*, declaring without much confidence that Carmen's friends were his—or her—friends and that we were all welcome if we'd like to join the "family."

The family?

Manon acted as if he didn't know François, conspicuously avoiding his gaze and his outstretched hand. It was crude, obvious, and a little embarrassing. A love affair that had gone sour? An acknowledged desire that one of them, most likely François, had refused to submit to? François was displaying something that looked more like a snicker than a smile, maybe that was what was so insulting to the doorman.

Alan leaned across to me with his hand on my forearm.

"Es-tyu déjà venyu ici, toi?"

"No, I've never been here. How about you?"

"No. And I'm not sure I want to go in ... "

It was my turn to cling to him.

"Don't leave me! I don't know what's inside and it's scary."

After Pinocchio, I'd just turned into Hansel and Gretel discovering the wicked witch's rock candy house ... Who knows, in the midst of the pandemonium maybe there was a cage for little children and an oven to cook them in, Tropical-style. Maybe I'd leave there feeling nostalgic about my innocence.

That was when François did the most amazing thing. Just before we walked in the door, he shoved his guitar into my arms.

"Will you hold this for me, please?"

"Why?"

"Never mind why! I'd like you to look after it while we're inside ... "

"Are you nuts? What am I supposed to do with a guitar? I don't even know how you're supposed to hold it!"

"I'm just asking you a favour."

"Check it in the cloakroom."

"There isn't one."

"So stand it in a corner."

"I'd never find it again!"

"Listen, did you just bring me here so I could hold your goddamn guitar? I'm not your employee! Besides, you can carry it by yourself!"

"They don't know I'm a singer ... "

"What?"

"I've never told them ... And maybe they wouldn't approve ... "

"What do you mean, wouldn't approve! Haven't they ever seen a guitar?"

"Yes, but they tend to look down their noses at *chansonniers* ... "

I was so shocked that all that emerged from my mouth was nonsense, like my mother when I went too far and she started to babble.

"You ... You're the most talented *chansonnier* I've ever seen ... and ... and you ... you ... you hang out with people who don't like it! You're ... you're out of your mind! Why not stay with your ... with your friends at El Cortijo?"

François' handsome face was right up against mine; I could see in his eyes the answer that was coming, that I didn't want to hear.

"When you get to know the Tropical, you'll understand ... I can't get along without what goes on there, and I'm not part of the family yet ... If I want them to accept me I have to act like them ... "

So he was also desperate to be accepted by a group!

Carmen had stuck his head inside the door and there was an ironic smile on his pretty face.

"Come on, lovebirds, come inside if you want to kiss, it's warmer."

*

Inside, the Tropical looked a little like the Quatre Coins du Monde or, I assumed, any place like it anywhere in the world—a bar, some tables, smoke, and alcohol fumes— but its clientele was less reserved than those at the Stanley Street club, and the atmosphere was more playful. The games played there were very different, though, the forbidden kind, the kind that I for one had never seen before, and I stood there gawking, nearly scandalized at the sight of two male or two female couples dancing in one another's arms, with indecent passion, while cruising raged out of control around the crowded dance floor.

At the other bar everything was done on the sly, with shame and discretion, except during the ultimate moments after last call when the final barriers had given way to the force of despair. Here, couples formed and fell apart with a coolness that thrilled the libertine I wanted to become, while shocking the Judaeo-Christian I still was.

Which was also what I'd come looking for, of course, and I'd found it after many peregrinations, but I wasn't altogether sure now that I was ready for it, like a too-rich dessert after a copious meal. Now fear of disappointment was added to the excitement at having finally reached my destination. What if in the end it was as boring as everything else? My return to the woes of *Manon Lescaut* or *Cenerentola* would only be hastened—and most likely final ...

Needless to say I stood there with François' guitar in my arms. This time he'd handed it over without asking, then disappeared with his tame dwarf who was bragging about introducing him to La Monroe—probably a transvestite with a little too much weight who'd seen *Some Like It Hot* and thought that if Marilyn could carry a few extra pounds, so could he—whom he'd seen going discreetly into the wings, looking conspiratorial.

The first transvestites I'd ever seen had wiggled and wriggled before my eyes for a good ten minutes before I realized they were men. They'd chattered, danced, flirted— without rousing my suspicions in the least; or Alan's either for that matter, who was if anything more naive than me. He was sipping a beer—I'd refused one and was nursing a warm, flat Seven-Up—and, like me, wondering what all those women were doing in a homosexual bar ...

It was the not always very feminine voices of these beauties who laid on the Max Factor with a trowel and great sacrifice that finally got me thinking ... I was so stunned, realizing just in time that I was holding the guitar too tightly and was liable to break it if I wasn't more careful. I'd seen Guilda on TV like everybody else and I thought she was gorgeous and very good, but I didn't know you could dress up like that in real life, just for fun on a Saturday night, to go dancing downtown! What a bizarre idea!

Because of the goddamn guitar that got in my way and probably too because Alan and I had been gawking at them for too long, I'd finally become the target of heckling that luckily for me had soon dissipated into simple bitching between girlfriends.

"Look at that, girls. Félix Junior's looking under our skirts for inspiration! He's going to compose a a new version of "Moi, mes souliers"—except that his will have high-heels."

"Don't worry, darling, the *chanteur* isn't looking for inspiration, what he wants is perspiration!"

I was as red as a poppy and cursing François for making me look like what I wasn't while he was having fun with a manly Marilyn and a Carmen dressed up like James Dean.

"Marc Gélinas or Hervé Brousseau aren't coming tonight, they just send us their burrs!"

This time I went white with rage and dreamed of yanking the wig off the insolent person who'd called me a burr; maybe I wasn't very handsome but I sure as hell wasn't a burr!

"Why should they turn up? They aren't interested in us. They're straighter than my father!"

"Actually, Veronika, I saw your father in the toilet at the train station the other night! Since when do straights do the limbo between the stalls in a public toilet?"

(Wow, his father too? That's incredible!)

"Oh yeah? Well I saw yours outside the Normand Tavern on Mont-Royal this afternoon ... And that's a lot worse, cause it's true!"

(Ah—so it was a joke! This gang doesn't pull punches!)

While very instructive, my first contact with transvestites was far from a triumph ...

"Would you like to dance?"

I'd jumped because Alan's mouth was too close to my ear and he'd thought he had to shout.

"With the guitar? We'll look like fools!"

"Never mind the guitar."

"I can't ... If you recall, it was entrusted to me by the genius of El Cortijo."

"The genius of *what*?"

"Never mind, it would take too long to explain ... "

Then I realized that he'd just asked me to dance. A guy had asked me to dance! A guy I'd thought was handsome ever since I'd spotted him nearly a week before at the box office of Her Majesty's, whom I'd been having some not very kosher dreams about, was asking me to throw myself into his arms in the middle of a crowd that must have seen worse. Wasn't that something! And I had to say no because of a musical instrument belonging to another guy, who couldn't care less about me and whom I'd have liked to strangle—when I didn't feel like jumping on him and submitting him to my wildest desires (that's right, once again I'd come up too late with the right thing to say, some humour, some irony to keep from being too disappointed).

"You aren't tempted?"

My eyes locked with his and in a voice more like supplication than a simple wish to explain:

"Sure I'm tempted ... a lot—but see, I promised François I'd keep an eye on his guitar ... "

Suddenly, the object of my resentment had left my arms; Alan had stood it against the wall, behind an empty chair *and I didn't give a damn*! While I was holding it, it had been sacred, but now that someone else had taken the initiative and rid me of it, it could be stolen, chopped into a thousand pieces, sliced thin and turned into confetti—I didn't give a good goddamn!

Alan came back, smiling at me, and I became aware of what kind of music had just begun.

A slow dance, needless to say: perfect timing.

But how do two guys dance together? Did one of us lead, and if so which one? Did we have to talk about it, decide on the spot before the music was over, draw straws?

I draped my coat over the back of the chair to more or less hide the guitar. If it disappeared, my ten-dollar debt would be multiplied by ten and I didn't feel like begging on the streets of Montreal in mid-winter so I could pay François back.

Once we were on the dance floor, Alan simply took me in his arms and I went along with it. Totally. He was holding me by the waist and I automatically put my arms around his neck, as if I'd been doing it all my life.

(Beware of tacky sentiment, remember your sense of the ridiculous before you turn sickly sweet. Shut up! Enjoy the moment! It'll never come back. Never again will it be the first time.)

This physical abandon was something I hadn't known before. I had given in hundreds of times to other sorts of spells—to brilliant works by artists I revered—but that came through the eyes or ears, it was mainly through my eyes and ears that I'd succumbed to pleasure (the duet by Leonie Rysanek and George London in the second act of *The Flying Dutchman*; the cheese symphony in Zola's novel *The Belly of Paris*; the crossing of the Beresina in *War and Peace*; the death of Dido; absolutely everything by Matisse and Vermeer)—but now, for the first time in my life, all five senses were involved in the ultimate pleasure and I was dreaming that I could stay there, in Alan's arms, for the rest of my life, counting them one by one and appreciating them, individually or in a group.

My eyes were taking in the reddish hairs at the base of his neck, my tongue was tasting the prickly wool of his jacket, my fingers dared to wander in his hair, I listened to his breathing—I was sure I could hear his heart beat, and my nose had quite naturally found his left armpit. God but it smelled good! A redhead's prickly sweat filled my nostrils and I was taking it in great overwhelming gulps. How could something that was so unpleasant in any other circumstances become so wonderful? I could have drunk his armpit!

And, the normal crowning achievement of the event—two superb erections met through our pants.

If I'd been the only one in that state, I think I'd have died of shame; but the undeniable proof that Alan was just as excited reassured me and I was loving this unique moment, savouring it in the hope that it would last a long, long time (slow dances were reputed to be always too short, according to my friends who were already doing them).

When the piece was over—too soon indeed—we stood there embracing while the other couples separated. What to do? Wait for it to pass? But such things can't be controlled, especially not by excitable young men experiencing their first serious adventure (which was true of me in any case). If we had separated at the same time as the other couples we'd have probably been able to go unnoticed, but now it was too late, we were the only ones still on the dance floor, and I was positive that everyone's eyes were on us because everyone knew!

I wasn't altogether wrong: a transvestite who must have been watching us and could sense our embarrassment, summed up in a few words and with a shrug worthy of the worst Hollywood mannerisms—Bette Davis and Joan Crawford were always right up there in the hierarchy of imitations—the extremely embarrassing situation that Alan and I were in.

"Another couple of kiddies that can't control their little green shafts!"

Indeed, how could we face the other dancers in the state we were both in? I was beginning to miss my winter coat, but I'd have looked even weirder if I'd worn my heavy overcoat to dance in.

More rhythmical music had just started up, a remnant of the time not so long ago, in the fifties, when the mambo and the cha-cha-cha were wreaking havoc all over North America; the other dancers were wriggling on the floor as if they were in a ballroom dancing competition, but Alan and I just stood there fitted together, unmoving, drowned in our inextricable awkwardness. I hoped that we at least looked as if we were passionately in love. But some snickers suggested the opposite and I sighed with an exasperation that my partner could feel on his neck.

As usual, he made the first move.

"This ... it ... This is the first time it's happened to me ... You?"

Was he really referring to *that*—or to the fact that we'd just finished dancing a slow dance cheek to cheek?

As usual and out of sheer cowardice, I was evasive.

"Umm ... yeah—me too."

(You moron! Your prick's about to explode on his right thigh and you act like nothing's happening! Are you planning to stay there till morning because you know your hard-on will last until then?)

We must have been thinking exactly the same thing, both of us showering ourselves with insults, because after thirty seconds that seemed to go on for hours, our heads straightened up at the same time and exclaimed in a perfect unison worthy of the most magnificent of Mozart's duets, each with his own accent too, which added even more to the music:

"We can't just stand here like this. We have to do something!"

A wonderful big healthy laugh came from my throat, I felt my heart come undone all at once; Alan, as an Anglo-Saxon less accustomed to conveying his relief to all and sundry, contented himself with a smile sparkling with freckles.

Together, yet without consulting each other, we came apart as naturally as anything, exhibiting to everyone quite openly the undeniable proof of our mutual attraction.

The transvestites, who must have been informed of our predicament, were laughing at our adventure while saying nothing themselves (for a seasoned transvestite, having nothing at all to say on any subject betokens astonishment that belongs on the honour roll of exceptional events—and a humiliation difficult to overcome) and we walked past them without even putting our hands over our flies.

(If a cop sees us will we spend the night in jail? Too bad! And meanwhile, it's too much fun!)

But embarrassment returned when we got to the chair my winter coat was draped on. Should I discreetly hide myself or—clearly more appealing—sneak a look at Alan's expression of interest while at the same time showing off my own?

Then I remembered that we hadn't even kissed yet, probably too embarrassed by the chain of events that were coming so quickly. I regretted it even as I was plotting to remedy the situation as soon as possible.

Would he taste reddish-brown in the same way he smelled it? Ah—to rediscover that smell in his mouth ...

Alan was obviously trying to regain his composure.

"I'm thirsty. How about another Seven-Up?"

"Yes, please ... but this one's on me ... "

"No, no, you don't have to ... "

"I insist ... "

"No, no ... "

"Look! We aren't going to fight over it, okay!"

Before I set off in search of a waiter, with my ten-dollar bill in my hand, he whispered in my ear:

"If you want me to dance with you again, take off that ... that bone around your neck, it dug into my chest when we were dancing ... "

He took a few steps, came back.

"But keep the other one!"

*

Not one person that evening had appreciated my marrow-bone! I wanted to look artistic but all I looked was tacky. I took it off with a certain regret. *I* liked it. I liked the way it looked against my green sweater, a pale, round lunar spot against the dark wool, the slight pressure against my chest, the surprised way people looked at it—particularly that, of course. But—first small concession to a nascent love?—I didn't want it to annoy Alan. True, he hadn't said he found it ugly, but the mere thought that the small fragment of a skeleton had bothered him when we danced together made it less indispensable to me, so I rolled it up on its leather thong and the only criticism I could make was that the lace was a little too thick for the bone, which it should have enhanced but which actually masked it— before I slipped it into the pocket of my coat.

I'd try it at school, then we'd see ...

(Are you crazy? Planning to get yourself killed? They'd find you at the back of the recreation room with the lace around your neck and the bone rammed down your throat!)

"Where'd you put my guitar?"

In my agitation I hadn't seen François coming. His suspicious tone pissed me off intensely.

"I sold it to a transvestite who wanted to make it into an earring!"

The dwarf and the man in eye-shadow who were with François had a good laugh. He was offended and raised his voice.

"I didn't ask you to make jokes to look good to my friends, I asked you a simple question!"

"I didn't wait for an introduction to your friends before looking good, you know! I actually existed before tonight, I didn't just come to life the first time you looked at me!"

I picked up the guitar and held it at arm's length the way he'd done at the Quatre Coins du Monde when he spotted Carmen.

"And I could tell you what to do with your guitar but it would hurt and you'd like it too much!"

(That was a good one! You're learning, you're learning!)

Encouraged by the second burst of laughter I'd just provoked, I kept at it.

"I thought you didn't want anyone here to see you with it!"

He yielded, bending his head towards me, and said confidentially:

"That's all changed. The guy who was supposed to do the show got drunk and vamoosed with yesterday's take ... They asked me to replace him ... !"

"A while ago you didn't want them to know that you've got a guitar, now you're going to show it off to everybody on the stage! Are you crazy, they'll kill you ... "

"La Monroe swore that they wouldn't ... "

"Ah, so the famous Monroe ... "

"He's an *amazing* guy ... Listen, I'll explain it all later, right now I have to do my third show of the evening!"

"You must be done-in."

"Nope, not a bit. They gave me something to keep me awake till next Saturday!"

(Now drugs on top of everything else! Prince Charming—at least the first one who turned up—was a junkie!)

Alan came back with two Seven-Ups.

A little smile appeared on François' lips (already I was less sensitive to it, that was reassuring ...)

"By the way, how's it going with your admirer?"

"He's not my admirer."

"Oh yes he is and in two weeks you'll be married to the eyeballs!"

The individual called La Monroe placed a be-ringed hand on François' shoulder and he turned towards her at once, as if I no longer existed.

"You'd better start, dear, before people get fed up and leave ... I don't mind running a blind pig, but it has to be worth my while!"

As if it were the funniest remark in the world, the most brilliant witticism, Carmen the dwarf burst out laughing, slapping his thighs. La Monroe sighed with exasperation.

"Carmen, will you stop laughing at everything I say! People will think I pay you!"

The dwarf slapped his thigh even harder, exclaiming:

"They'll think I pay you! That's a good one! Did you hear that? They'll think I pay you!"

Far from the fat transvestite I'd expected, La Monroe was a long and lanky nervous beanpole, an agitated pack of bones, half-man and half-woman—a hybrid in fact, somewhere between a woman in pants like Barbara Stanwyck, whom you expect to pull a revolver out of her purse at the first opportunity, and the half-disguised and therefore more grotesque man à la Jack Lemmon in certain scenes from *Some Like It Hot*. His eyes were very intelligent and when he spoke, you knew right away who you were dealing with: the whole cruel but amazingly knowing side of him that years of experience in a world without pity bestowed on the texture of a voice made itself felt in his every word and I told myself that being one of his enemies would not be a barrel of laughs. Better watch your step around him if you wanted to be unscathed.

And Carmen the dwarf was the blatant truth of that. He was such an ass-kisser in front of La Monroe, it made him loathsome. He reacted to *every word* she said, repeated it to be sure that everyone appreciated it, even went so far as to mimic its meaning or, at least, the effect it was supposed to produce, which made his face look like a Christmas tree with too many lights on, about to cause a power failure. La Monroe was his blessed mother, his idol, his goddess, he worshipped her absolutely—and wanted it known. He wanted to be liked for it, he was dying for his idol to notice him or at least to be even the slightest bit aware of his existence. The goddess obviously wasn't taken in and she treated him with insulting contempt.

A foreign body in this unusual group, Alan merely nodded at everything that was said, without really following the conversation. Once the three weirdos had left—with Carmen trotting behind his Pygmalion like a little doggy—the two of us were there in a tête-à-tête and he didn't have the faintest idea what had happened.

"Why are they leaving?"

"François's going to sing."

"Here?"

"Yes."

"Does he sing rock 'n' roll?"

"No, and that's the problem."

There was a hubbub coming from the side of the stage—if this was François' third performance, it was also mine!—some lights went out and something approaching silence fell over the bar. Alan took me by the waist in a move that was perfectly natural and my crotch, which had calmed down a little in the past few minutes, blossomed again.

"Have you heard him sing?"

"Yes."

"Is he good?"

"He's fabulous."

"What does he sing?"

"His own songs."

"With just a guitar?"

"Yes."

"Like Elvis when he was starting out?"

"I guess so. But what he sings is really different. It's more like ... how can I put it ... folksongs? No, not like folksongs but ... you know ... the kind of songs that don't swing?"

"But this is no place to do that!"

"I know."

"Does he?"

"Yup."

"And he's singing anyway?"

"Right."

"They'll kill him!"

"That's right!"

La Monroe walked onto the stage as if she were at home, unannounced and very much the businesswoman, with one hand on her hip and the other one kneading her lower lip—the very image of a boss with a serious problem to resolve who wants to tell her staff.

She got a warm welcome, more friendly than admiring, and I realized that La Monroe really was just the boss, that she didn't perform on stage so that inevitably she wasn't wreathed in the halo of a great star or those who imitate them. In real life she must be very impressive, but the stage was not her realm, she gladly left it to the performers who entertained her audience while she counted the cash in the wings.

"Quiet please, Mama's got something to tell you ... "

Only Carmen reacted, laughing too hard. La Monroe couldn't help giving him a filthy look. Instead of feeling threatened, the dwarf was flattered. Poor Carmen, he didn't know that he was going to get an earful before long—or he was acting as if he didn't ...

"I've got good news and bad news."

A disappointed murmur ran through the room. I heard a nearby transvestite whisper: "Tallulah's paid another visit to the kingdom of Johnny Walker ... No show tonight ... "

La Monroe went on however, raising her arms like Norma when she starts singing her famous "Casta Diva"—or as she does in Maria Callas photos.

"You know that every Saturday night after last call I ask a few hundred of my nears and dears to stay for one last show—and one last drink ... After all, the protection money I pay the police has to be used for something ... "

Some laughs. Not many.

"Tonight, alas, our very own Tallulah—who was supposed to tell us about the latest disappointments in her love life as only she can do—is indisposed ... "

At this, many more laughs, a wave of complicity that contained as much mockery as sympathy, along with a hint of appreciative commiseration as a bonus ... It wasn't the first time Tallulah had let her public down for the same reason and her public, though disappointed, forgave her.

" ... So the Tropical had to find a replacement fast, at a moment's notice ... "

The curiosity went up a notch. There was going to be a show after all.

Still the same transvestite:

"Mind you we could do with a change ... Poor Tallulah, she's great when she's in good shape, but in the past few months the bottle has definitely replaced her muse."

To describe François, La Monroe had opted for the lyrical, probably to prepare her flock for a performance of a kind they weren't used to.

"First of all, he's very handsome, which doesn't hurt; after that, he's a poet, a very young poet, a very *handsome* and very young poet who composes his own songs and sings them ... accompanied by his guitar like that guy in Greek mythology ... what's his name ... Morpheus, that's right, Morpheus and Eurydice ... "

Around me, frowning and shrugging.

"Murphy who?"

It didn't look good.

"Tonight you will be witnessing the birth of a great talent, so I'd like to ask you not to behave like boors ... "

Not one laugh. Sniffing danger, La Monroe swallowed her gum.

"So without further delay—the young man who's already being seen as the potential heir of our great Félix Leclerc—will you please welcome François Villeneuve!"

At the name of Félix Leclerc, a shudder of horror had run through the crowd and La Monroe realized—too late—that she'd made a gaffe. That name was not to be uttered on a stage normally occupied by wannabe Josephine Bakers and Mae Wests. Cursing she disappeared backstage.

Only appreciative whistles for his appearance greeted François when he came on. Every man there would have fucked him on the spot, he was so beautiful in the flattering pink spotlight, and I told myself that if Alan hadn't been beside me I'd have once again died of jealousy (one small hint of it remained anyway, an annoying little drop in pressure that I tried to chase away by taking refuge with my nose under Alan's arm who tensed up, probably wondering what I was doing there.) I had to convince myself once and for all that my Prince Charming was not the one I'd first thought and that unfortunately the battle wasn't over yet.

The next few minutes were a nightmare. This crowd, accustomed to thundering music and crude gags didn't give François a chance and he was in agony.

The first song was greeted with surprise and relative silence—a bar is never totally silent. There were even a few laughs: they thought it was a joke, they were expecting that at any moment the handsome singer would produce a mouth-fart or come out with some insanity that would make them all explode with laughter, but the song—though very beautiful and moving—unfurled with no comic interruption, and the audience was stupefied to realize that this was the price to be paid that evening to go on drinking after hours.

And then the pandemonium promised by the dwarf really did explode.

The transvestite beside me—he must have been the spokesman for his group who'd gathered behind him—started by making a sound of disappointment with his tongue (tsk tsk tsk), a little like my mother when she was depressed at what was being offered on TV, then added in a loud voice:

"Shit, I came here to unwind, not to concentrate! It's too late to concentrate, me and the night are too far gone."

He was absolutely right. That song wasn't intended for a place like this and François had been presumptuous to think he could capture the attention of a crowd who'd been drinking for hours and wanted some laughs before they went to bed. Those who weren't having sex by now wouldn't have sex at all. The thought of it threw me into a panic. I'd lost sight a little of tonight's goal and I caught myself wondering to whom I was going to surrender my virginity—if I did actually surrender it. I tried to picture Alan naked and all I saw was a shock of red hair.

At the foot of the stage, the Tropical's boss was looking furiously at Carmen: he must have been the one who recommended François to replace Tallulah and the martyrdom he'd have to endure would be phenomenal. He knew it and he started to play the quivering little chihuahua trying to attract his mistress's pity.

Bravely, François got to the end of his song without reacting to the signs of exasperation now coming thick and fast.

He was booed, but with his boundless pride he had the gall to smile and take a bow, then launch into a second song. Which we could barely hear over the whistling and jeering. After the triumph at El Cortijo, where every intellectual in Montreal was at his feet, drinking in his words, and seeing him as the future of Québécois song, this monumental flop in front of a boozy crowd must have been terrible and heart-breaking. I moved away from Alan a little as if I were going to defend François. Or save him. Alan held onto my fingertips.

"We should go before things get worse."

Onstage, François laid down his arms. With a wicked look he watched the crowd insult him. In his fury he was more gorgeous, more sexy that ever.

"You fucking ignoramuses! You're going to hear about me some day and you'll be sorry you didn't listen to me tonight! But don't you dare beg me to come back! Never!"

He jumped off the stage and made his way towards us, clearing a path with his elbows and his guitar. He wasn't going to deliberately destroy his livelihood!

"Come on. We're leaving."

It was not a suggestion, but an order. I was about to point out that Alan and I weren't there to serve him even though he was having a rough time, when the transvestite who'd started the conspiracy leaned over to us—he was over six feet tall without the wig—and kindly laid a hand on François' shoulder.

"What happened isn't our fault, darling, it's yours! You never should have walked onto that stage with that material. I myself wouldn't dare and I want it to be my profession. What they want here is Mae West, darling, they want glamour and fantasy—not Gilles Vigneault!"

François looked at him; for a moment I thought he was going to claw his eyes out. He was like one of those spoiled brats who aren't used to being told no and who go ballistic at the slightest provocation. He looked almost ugly with his mouth pinched, his nose flattened and his brow creased, and I asked myself with a hint of concern whether that might be his real nature, usually kept under wraps the better to seduce.

His voice was expressionless and icy, much more terrible than any outright anger.

"Move that hand or you'll be climbing onto the stage to look for it! I've got pointed teeth and powerful jaws and I love the sight of blood!"

I think the transvestite really believed him because he sat there gawking for the second time in less than half an hour. And his hand disappeared behind his back as if François had just told him it had wrinkles.

I'd barely had time to put on my coat when I felt myself being shaken by the sleeve.

"Bring your Anglo if you want, but move it!"

I felt I'd gone a little too quickly from boundless admiration to shameful contempt—was this my Prince Charming, this pitiful temperamental child who couldn't endure the slightest setback? But I followed François without a word, pulling my Anglo by the hand.

PRINCE CHARMING ISN'T ALWAYS
THE ONE YOU THINK: LUCKILY!

François stood on the sidewalk on Peel Street, in a rage.

"I can't believe I was dying to be accepted by those retards! I'm an idiot! And blind! A wimp!"

Carmen, probably banished by his goddess and already looking for a new master to flatter basely in the hope of even a glancing, contemptuous caress, tried his best to console him.

"Don't let it get you down, François ... I'm sure La Monroe isn't pissed off with you, and ... "

"I don't give a shit if she is or she isn't! I just don't ever want to see that face again—that face like a horse with fever! Do you think I'll ever set foot in there again after what just happened? Are you crazy? Are you sick? You don't know me! I'll step in shit once—then I go out of my way to avoid it! And I've got a steel-trap memory! And one hell of a knack for bearing a grudge! And don't even mention revenge!"

Alan and I were standing in the background. My knee, which I'd more or less forgotten in my excitement and my first real sexual turmoil, was again making its presence felt. The humid air was seeping inside my coat and my pants, I'd had enough, I wanted to leave, disappear, forget. My bed! What I wouldn't give for my bed! A headache was starting to bore into my temples—fatigue or stress or the two at once ...

Alan was standing very close to me, his arm around my waist, as if he'd suddenly realized that he risked losing me from one second to another because I was probably going to hop in the first taxi that drove up and disappear from his life forever.

I didn't want to leave him either. The lingering warmth in my cheeks and the memory of a huge erection still held sway over me, even though I was numb from exhaustion, but I could not imagine what might come next, what could turn up in the minutes to come to save this night from utter disaster and bitter disappointment. As usual, I would have preferred to withdraw without taking any initiative, even if it meant seeming like a quitter, like the asshole I was.

"I guess I'll go home ... "

"Where's that?"

"Why do you ask?"

"Just to know ... to continue our conversation ... because I don't want us to separate just like that ... "

(Go on, take the plunge! Ask the Big Question! Close your eyes if you think it will be easier that way!)

"How about you, where do you live?"

"A long way from here ... "

"What does that mean, a long way from here?"

"It means Pointe-Saint-Charles. Do you know where that is?"

An Anglo who lives in Pointe-Saint-Charles! Not Westmount! Not even Outremont! A poor Anglo! So Alan must have bought cheap tickets because he didn't have much money, not for the reason I believed.

"Pointe-Saint-Charles? ... No. I just know it's in the western part of the island ... somewhere around ... I don't know ... around Lachine? Verdun? Saint-Henri?"

"You don't seem to know Montreal very well."

"How well do you know the Plateau-Mont-Royal?"

"No, it's true, you're right ... All I know is that it's in the east ... around ... around the Faubourg à Mélasse, Little Burgundy, Rosemont?"

It felt good to laugh in the midst of this maelstrom of racing around, of comings and goings, of being on the wrong track, of abandoned hopes and semi-disappointments ... François, of course, wasn't happy.

"If you want to make fun of me, do it to my face, maybe I'll join in!"

· I was officially fucking fed up.

I hurled myself at him and told him straight to his face as he'd asked:

"Okay, enough! Do you think you're so important that you're all anybody talks about? There's a whole planet out there, sweetheart! There's you on one side and three billion more on the other! So how about leaving some air for the other three billion? Alan and I are trying to find a way to spend the night together, that's no concern of yours and it's no *business* of yours!"

I was amazed at what had just come out of my mouth and I didn't dare turn around to face Alan for fear he'd reject me on the grounds of grave indiscretion.

(Now you've done it, the big question's been asked—but you've asked the wrong person! Goddamn nitwit!)

Amazed at my own belligerence and still too worked-up to find a pithy formula that would shut me up, François changed tack, probably in the hope of defusing the animosity that was rising between us as clear as day.

"Hey, did you put Seven-Up in your beer? Your breath smells weird ... but it's not bad ... "

That lightened the atmosphere a little—Carmen was laughing too hard and I could see what a handsome couple he'd form with François—and I was able to face my admirer, as the singer had christened him, while I foraged in my coat pocket for gum ...

François had had time to perk up and use his wits.

"Where were you? Had you got to, Your place or mine? or were you too shy to go there, which is what I think?"

Then a very amusing thought seemed to strike him and he asked us with fake innocence:

"Tell me—by any chance are the two of you virgins?"

Both our faces, which went from the-party's-over-pale to beet red in less than three seconds, spoke volumes. Carmen nearly collapsed with laughter on the icy Peel Street sidewalk, François took on the look—half-contrite, half-fake-sorry—of someone whose nasty crack, though dreamed up on the spur of the moment, had been too close to the bone—and now he wanted to be forgiven.

"I'm sorry ... I didn't intend to be *that* on target. Do you want some advice? Do you want me to draw a picture? Do you want me to guide you? Do you want me to play Mr. Experience and do a threesome? Or a quartet—because Carmen's pretty well clued-in too."

Carmen was shrieking so loud I was sure the police were on their way. Meanwhile, our problem was far from solved.

(Good for me, falling for somebody as inexperienced as I was. It's going to be lovely if neither of us knows what to do! Oh well—we'll let nature take her course, she's supposed to know everything!)

Ignoring the other two, who were having too much fun at our expense—I thought that François had too quickly forgotten his own all too recent trials and tribulations, which just a few minutes earlier it had seemed he'd never survive—I leaned across to Alan who seemed to be on the verge of tears.

"We can't go to my place, Alan. I live with my parents. I saw you with your mother at the opera tonight—do you live at home too?"

He gave a little nod and I cursed to myself.

So there you go, the end of the story. All that to arrive at such a point, at an unavoidable cul-de-sac where my virginity would remain intact despite all my efforts.

Once again—this was definitely a night for surprises—salvation came from an unexpected quarter.

François had taken out a ring of keys that he held aloft like the Statue of Liberty with her torch.

"I've got the keys to El Cortijo. There's a nice deep sofa in the back room ... I'm offering you your first night of love even if you don't deserve it ... And I don't know why I said that, you deserve it as much as anybody else ... "

I'd lifted my finger like a little boy at school.

"Where will you be when we're there?"

That beautiful smile again, and a pinch in my heart though it was officially otherwise engaged.

"For want of bread, we eat cake; for want of giants, we devour dwarves!"

It was terribly cruel but Carmen took it as a compliment and nearly collapsed with gratitude, excitement and expectation.

It was Alan's turn to lean across to me.

"Where does he want to take us? And how many sofas did he say there are?"

*

At first, the taxi driver refused to take four passengers and only the promise of a lavish tip made him change his mind.

"I won't go far, I'm warning you! This is my last trip of the night, I'm going home to bed! Don't make me drive all over Montreal, I'm going to *one* place, even if there's four of you!"

"As a matter of fact we're all going to the same address."

"All four of you? That must be quite a house!"

François obviously didn't want a hard time from a cabbie.

"Just shut up and drive!"

"So he gets into a cab outside a bar for queers and he wants to pass for a man!"

"Have you ever been undressed by four fucking queers? No? Then shut up and get moving!"

The thought must have really disgusted him because he simply muttered between his teeth and drove.

The dashboard clock showed seven minutes past four. As soon as we were settled on the fake leather seat, a feeling that went far beyond physical fatigue descended on every one of my bones, each of my fibres and my brain as well. I wasn't exhausted, I was devastated, like a battlefield after a particularly vicious attack. The thought that in a few minutes I would be obliged to provide a sexual performance—my very first and maybe the most important, because it would be decisive—defeated me. To sleep in Alan's arms, yes; to bury my nose in his neck, breathe in his body all night long, feel his interest in me, gently unfold my own, if need be go as far as intimate caresses with no repercussions, fine, but the prospect of going all the way without really knowing what awaited me—is it very painful the first time, would I hurt Alan?— trying to regain my equilibrium in the midst of some complex gymnastics when I didn't have the full use of my head—or my body, for that matter, because I knew that I couldn't use my left knee—puffing and panting while waiting for the great shudder and the cathartic cry, to watch Alan—already russet—turn as red as a poppy and to feel myself on the verge of apoplexy—was throwing me into a panic all at once, and I wasn't at all sure that fatigue was the only reason.

And what if I quite simply wasn't ready to make the big leap?

(Seems to me these things should happen when you're in shape, not when you're tired half to death! If I'm no good, if he's no good either, what will we do? Lie there and gawk at the ceiling? What does the El Cortijo ceiling look like anyway? Are there fishnets like in the other clubs, other *boîtes à chansons*? I don't think so ... Usually I notice things like that, but ... Don't change the subject, you know perfectly well the El Cortijo ceiling is of no importance now ...)

While the taxi was making its way along Ontario Street—slowly because of the ice—I had to face facts: I was afraid of being afraid of sex.

What's more, Alan had fallen asleep on my shoulder!

*

I didn't have time to explain to Alan what El Cortijo was, so he frowned a little as the four of us stood on the Clark Street hill after we'd paid off the taxi.

"Another bar?"

"Another kind, yes ... "

Amazingly, I was not surprised when François noticed that the café door wasn't locked. I was even relieved at the thought that someone was still there and that in the end, I was going to have to quietly make my way home.

François stammered some apologies as he pushed open the door.

Françoise Berd, André Pagé and Tex were at a table talking, over a bottle of red wine. Instead of having the effect of a bomb, our arrival seemed to make everybody happy. Tex, ever the gentleman, got up, exclaiming:

"Greetings, artiste, to what do we owe the privilege?"

André and Françoise also seemed overjoyed. She was wiping her face as if she'd been laughing too hard.

As for François, he put on a mock-cheerful tone.

"What are you all doing here?"

"They turned up just as I was about to leave, and then one thing led to another ... "

François had gone to their table, leaving us stranded at the door. He spoke to Madame Berd with a touch of irony in his voice:

"Did you find your thief yet?"

Tex beckoned to us.

"Sit down and drink some wine, that'll warm you up!"

We entered shyly, like children at a grownups' party. I introduced Alan, François introduced Carmen, whom Tex already knew but who seemed to pique the curiosity of the other two. The wine was soon poured and I turned it down, I was too afraid even to taste it, I was too afraid that my nose would land in my glass and I'd drown.

While Françoise was speaking, Alan seemed stunned to have ended up where he was at that moment, in the company of some strange characters who were drinking red wine in a café that had been closed for hours and talking cheerfully about song-thieves and car chases across the city.

Despite her fatigue and her agitation, Madame Berd had lost none of her verve.

"So think of it, we chased him for nearly half an hour before we realized that it wasn't him after all! In fact we'd suspected it wasn't him but as I always tell André when he's laughing too hard at the ridiculous situation we're in: 'Even if he's not the one, it works off my frustration just to chase him! I feel as if I'm doing something, not just throwing in the towel. You know me, that's not my style! And if it was him, if it *was* him—you never know.' Luckily, I don't think the poor guy realized we were following him, he was too busy looking for an address ... "

She bent over slightly, added conspiratorially:

"Maybe we didn't find a song-thief but we did come across a drug dealer!"

André Pagé interrupted her.

"Françoise, we don't know for sure ... "

"Listen, a guy who stops at three addresses in half an hour ... "

"Maybe he was delivering barbecued chicken ... "

"There wasn't anything on his car ... "

"But he had a bunch of packages ... "

"Just as I said ... "

"Those packages were too big for drugs ... "

"If you were delivering drugs, wouldn't you disguise it as something else? Barbecued chicken, maybe?"

"So then we were scared he'd spot us—those guys always have to be on their toes—and we gave up the chase ... We played cops-and-robbers for half an hour: you can imagine how much I enjoyed it!"

Tex, who must have heard the story at least ten times, was still laughing.

"Maybe he was delivering Gilles Vigneault's songs!"

I could have told them that the fleet of trucks that had replaced me when I was fired by a barbecue joint a few years earlier were unidentified for weeks at first, because the people who did the lettering were busy elsewhere. Their suspect could indeed be the delivery boy for a new restaurant ... But that would have meant joining the conversation, telling them part of the story of my life, offering up explanations that would be long and, in the end, very uninteresting; anyway, I was too tired.

François wanted to know every detail.

"Why did you come back here instead of going home?"

André Pagé's broad and generous smile was reminiscent of François's; it must have wreaked a fair amount of havoc in Montreal's artistic circles.

"You know Françoise, she's sentimental ... She wanted to come back and check one last time before she went to bed, in case the thief, in a fit of remorse, had returned Gilles's briefcase."

"Where? On the street?"

"Or here, at the El."

Françoise sighed, shaking her head.

"If you ask me, that would be the only thing to do. You steal a car because you need it or you want to sell it, okay, but what do you do with a briefcase full of original songs?"

I put in my two cents' worth, maybe to console her.

"When they realize they're Gilles Vigneault's, maybe they'll try to sell them ... "

Madame Berd's eyes lit up as if she'd just seen the Virgin in her cave, saying: "Poor Canada!"

"You're right! I didn't think of that! You're a bright young man, you know! Good thing you came back here, I'll be able to sleep tonight. The songs may not be lost ... Maybe Gilles will be able to buy them back from the thief!"

Tex looked dubious.

"Maybe Gilles can't afford to buy them back ... I know that if somebody stole mine ... "

Madame Berd, who'd said it herself, wouldn't give in so easily.

"We'll all go in together and buy them back!"

I didn't believe it myself—nor did the others, for that matter, even if at four a.m. fairy tales sometimes seem real—but I was proud of my good deed. I felt as if I was making up for the fact that I'd never been a Boy Scout.

Then *the* question came, like a bolt from the blue, and all four of us fell silent. Tex had gotten up to get what he claimed would be one last bottle of wine and asked François, straight-faced but sure of his effect:

"You still haven't answered my question, Mr. Songsmith! Why have you come back here? Do you need my sofa again?"

The seconds that followed were very interesting. In the general silence, I had the impression that I was hearing each person think: François was looking for an excuse, Alan wanted to get the hell out, Carmen must have been enjoying the general malaise, and the other two, through cross-checking and deductions—and also through our crestfallen expressions—guessed our intentions and were hiding their smiles in their empty glasses.

François merely hung his head—chicken! He could have come up with a thousand reasons!—and we all looked like a failed orgy.

Alan got up.

"Excuse me ... I really have to go."

I copied him, though without a word.

Tex went around the table, sat us back down with friendly smacks on our backs that were strong enough to reverberate all the way to our heels, they were that vigorous.

"Come on, guys, it was a joke ... Sit down and finish your drinks at least! If you haven't got a place to sleep I'm leaving in a few minutes, the sofa's all yours ... But a sofa for four, I think it would be a little crowded ... Especially that one!"

Françoise and André chortled one last time as they got up.

"Okay, it's late, let's get moving."

The café emptied out in the time it took to say it (sincere hugs, warm handshakes, I hope we'll see each other again, thanks, Tex, that's really nice of you, you're welcome but let's not go overboard with the consecrated bread, no, no, it's the last time, so we say, so we say ...)

When the four of us were alone again, a silence heavy with various expectations and pointed questions fell over El Cortijo, which had been plunged into semi-darkness by François, who knew what he was doing. Though the moment didn't lend itself, I thought about my mother who'd probably been waiting up for me with her nose against the dining room window, worried sick. She must have called the police three or four times already, been laughed at because I was eighteen years old and I could do as I liked on Saturday night, been called a mother hen, she must have berated them on the telephone in her inimitable way, accusing them of being heartless and rude, then paced the whole house like a caged lion whose cub has been taken away, probably stuffing her face with chocolate cake—lucky her—for consolation, and realizing that it didn't work, it only intensified her anxiety and dealt another blow to her already congested liver.

It would be in my interest to take full advantage of the night because my homecoming was going to be explosive.

I had learned the word *pandemonium* in the course of the evening and for a few moments I revelled in portraying our apartment as the capital of Hell, starring Mama as a vociferous and ridiculous Lady Lucifer in a fire-red leather outfit, but really she's the salt of the earth and at the end of the day, quite merciful. Myself I cast as a naive neophyte who insists on visiting these premises instead of contritely tearing out my heart.

Needless to say—I knew it, I could have sworn, I'd have bet my life on it!—the sofa was too small for four. All that could happen there was an accelerated, overcrowded orgy that would generate some instant Judaeo-Christian remorse. Alan and I were so discouraged, so drunk with exhaustion, that without the kind heart of François, who could have taken advantage but who realized how miserable we were, we'd have let ourselves be cheated without a word, out of sheer exhaustion putting off till later, the enchanted night that we'd so much hoped for (at least I had).

"Have you got enough money to get home?"

I jumped because all four of us were facing the bed of sin, arms dangling and heads bowed, like children who'd misbehaved and were now lined up outside a confessional, whereas I was sure that the next sounds I heard would be the inexhaustible and inelegant stomach-rumbling generated by two bodies having sex—in my imagination at any rate.

"I've still got seven dollars of what you lent me."

A quick look at Alan who, like me, had realized he was on the edge of the abyss and still couldn't believe what he had narrowly missed.

"Me ... I ... "

Slowly he emptied his pockets; you might have thought he was drunk, he was staggering so much from fatigue and was obviously finding it hard to count his money.

"Yes ... I think so ... "

François had collapsed into the refractory springs that must have already stabbed him in the backside.

"Exchange phone numbers ... Promise you'll call each other back. Each of you take a taxi ... go home ... "

I could have clawed his face off. He'd kept me running all night and now he was telling me to go home like a good boy and go to bed—because it was bedtime! My two Prince Charmings were getting away from me. I'd travelled around the city twice for nothing! Not only would I have to face my mother with my cherry still intact, I would also have in the back of my throat the unpleasant aftertaste of a task not done, of letdown after vainly exhausting all my energies, of a stinging and humiliating failure that debilitates a person's self-esteem until it's less than nothing. If I let myself wax lyrical just a little bit more, my brain would explode and the sofa could never be used again as a trampoline for love!

I had gone out in search of supreme happiness and I'd be going home a bit like a beggar who's had a disastrous day.

François must have sensed my distress because he looked up at me with a sincerely sad expression—which was worse! I refused to give François the right to a hang-dog look!—shrugging helplessly.

But I was also refusing myself the grand break-up scene, the vitriolic rebuke, the violently precise insults, the threats so harrowing that the victim is afraid they'll be implemented. Because Alan was there, of course, himself the plaything of this disastrous evening, but even more of the blunting of my brain that would probably keep me from achieving the effects I'd aim at and would leave me frustrated.

For one quick moment I dreamed of writing to François as repayment of his loan—that was all the strength I had left—a letter so violent it would prevent him from having the career everyone was predicting for him—aside from the Tropical's regulars ... It wasn't much for such a big let-down but it relieved me all the same.

"I can call Diamond Taxi if you want ... "

"Never mind! I'd rather not ask you for anything. And if my knee didn't hurt so much I'd give you back your money so I'd never have to lay eyes on you again!"

"I understand."

"Like hell you do! You've had your fun, nothing else matters."

"You're wrong ... I haven't had *all* my fun ... "

I replied without thinking and I could have kicked myself, I felt so spiteful:

"You said it yourself: for want of giants ... "

A movement on my right. Carmen had stepped up to me. Was he going to bite my crotch as I deserved and spit it out with a grimace of disgust? (But wasn't it just as spiteful to think that his mouth was at the level of my crotch?)

His strange voice, surprisingly, had taken on some nearly comforting modulations instead of the aggressive tone I might have expected, as if he'd decided on his own to solve the problems of some people too clueless to find their own solutions.

"Do you really feel like going home?"

"Listen, don't make it worse by playing mother! You're right though ... Right now I'd rather jump off the Jacques Cartier Bridge than face what's probably waiting for me at home ... "

He turned towards Alan, who was sitting on a wobbly little table that threatened to collapse under his weight at any moment. I could already see the Monday headlines: *Anglophone Knocked Out by Drunken, Drug-crazed Beatniks in Clark Street Den*!

"What about you?"

"Me? I have the impression that Pointe-Saint-Charles is so far away, it's another country ... "

"We *always* have that impression ... "

"What?"

"Nothing, nothing ... But if I came up with a way for you to spend the night together ... "

Oh no, not again! Not the Good Samaritan! I had absolutely no intention of ending the night at the Dwarfs' Palace on Rachel Street, in a bed even narrower than El Cortijo's sofa, with the American tourists who start ringing the bell at ten a.m.!

"No thanks. I'll skip that offer ... "

But Alan had come up to me, very softly putting his mouth against my right ear.

"It's our last chance ... "

All the tenderness in the world was in those few words, spoken with an accent you could cut with a knife, but so sexy it made me shiver.

I turned my head in his direction. Look, even his eyes were reddish brown.

Carmen had lowered his voice, like someone confessing a very serious sin.

"There's a Tourist Room on Carré Saint-Louis ... In fact it's called the Saint-Louis Tourist Room ... It's cheap, it's clean ... Tell Jackie, she's the boss, that I sent you. Ask her for room 22. That's the biggest, most comfortable one. You could even walk, it's that close."

I looked François straight in the eye. Would you look at that: the blue had faded, his eyes were too pale at this hour of the night ...

"Okay, call Diamond Taxi."

"It's too close, he'll be furious ... "

"If we pool our money we should be able to give him a fat tip too."

*

"Are you old enough?"

"Old enough for what? To sleep?"

"Old enough to rent a room, that's what!"

"How old do you have to be to rent a room?"

"The age for what you're getting ready to do ... "

"How old do you have to be for that! The age when you're allowed to rent a room? We're going around in circles ... "

"Listen, smart-ass, do you want a room or don't you?"

"Do you want to rent me a room or don't you? You're the one asking the questions, not me! If you interrogate all your customers like that they mustn't come back very often! And they mustn't have much time left to do what they've come to do!"

"I don't always have to interview them! My customers aren't always little baby chicks like you, with your belly button not dry yet and your asshole glued shut!"

"Don't worry, if I could afford to unglue my asshole somewhere else I'd've done it!"

"You've got a smart answer for everything. I'd hate to be your mother! Poor woman!"

"Let me tell you something: if my mother could see me right now she wouldn't want to be my mother either!"

"And I'm telling you—if it wasn't Carmen that sent you, you'd be bleeding on the ice outside by now!"

Jackie wasn't blonde, she was albino! How could a woman so obviously black to begin with manage to be so pale? The pittance she earned renting rooms must be barely enough to keep her in peroxide. And since she worked all night, she felt obliged to look tanned and did it with makeup. Changing from swarthy to paleface, she'd turned out toasted platinum blonde. And as the nights were sometimes long when there weren't many customers, her consumption of cheap chocolates was unreasonable—a five-pound box of Lowney's next to the cash register was proof—and she proudly wore the consequences.

We'd had no trouble finding the Saint-Louis Tourist Room and the taxi-driver had dropped us at the door, wishing us a friendly "Good night, girls!" that made Alan blush again. The poor thing must have blushed more often this evening than he ever had before.

It was obviously the first time I'd gone to a Tourist Room and as I was climbing the steps to the reception desk I wondered how to approach the person in charge: should I ask for the price or say nothing and take a key? Did you have to pay in advance or not till morning, ask for towels like in French movies, hide your face in your coat or act as if you were a regular customer, or fill out a form? For the police, in the event of murder ...

"You're going to fill out this little form for me, young man!"

(Time to invent a phony name! And job! And age! A whole life! I hoped that Alan would think about doing the same.)

"You too, Red."

I didn't dare look at Alan while we filled out our little white cards. Anyway, I was too busy faking an ID that was marginally credible ... Especially because the only thing that came to mind was either funny or ridiculous. Or both.

(We're taking too long! We're taking too long and she's going to suspect we aren't writing our real names! You turkey, do you really think people who come here use their real names? Her records must be fiull of John Smiths and Jos Simards, with fake doctors and alleged lawyers!)

Jackie took both the cards—we kept our eyes on the box of chocolates and guilt was oozing out of every pore—looked at them, imperturbable, then murmured:

"George Sand, student ... and Donald O'Connor ... dancer. What a great night! A nineteenth-century writer and a Hollywood star!"

But a hint of a smile blossomed at the corner of her lips and a tremendous relief descended on us, like the Holy Ghost on the anxious apostles on Pentecost morning.

"Can we have room 22? Carmen told us to ask for it if it's available."

"Do you want a free bottle of champagne too? Mink safes? A striptease ... though that could get you over-excited and my kid brother's already taken ... "

She took a key from the board behind her. It must have been a slack evening because only two or three were missing. The key for room 22 though was still there.

"Here, take this and count yourself lucky that I'm not asking you for ID ... and pray to God there won't be a raid tonight!"

At these encouraging words—I could already see myself, handcuffed and asking the cops' permission to phone home so my mother could come and strangle me— we made our way to the varnished wooden stairs that went up to the second floor. It reeked of bug spray and fake-lemon furniture polish.

Alan was trembling a little.

"Scared?"

"No, but I'm so tired I can't help shaking ... "

His fatigue on top of mine—how promising!

Probably guessing that this was our first time, Jackie treated us quite generously: the room was spacious, clean, welcoming ... even though the dominant colours were blue and green! The height of irony: I was going to be having sex in the ugly set from *Romeo and Juliet*!

But one confusing detail drew my attention right away and an absolute, ultimate taboo took hold of the bed, despite the fact that it was quite inviting, or so I thought just then: the aqua chenille bedspread was identical to the one my parents had when I was a child. The same floral pattern faded from too many washings, the same complicated intertwined designs surrounding and choking the flowers, the same edging that was all twisted because it hadn't been sewn on properly in the first place, the same softness from overuse.

Drunk with exhaustion and ready to give in to the most morbid fantasies, I had a vision that it was the same one, a warning from beyond the bedspread, from the heaven of bedding, from the hell of old household objects that were coming back to exact revenge for the poor treatment they'd suffered, and I stood rooted in the middle of the room, mouth and eyes wide-open, convinced this time that nothing, absolutely nothing could happen between Alan and me tonight because my mother's old bedspread would witness it.

"Are you the one that's scared now?"

The bedspread was worn in the same places, though with some new spots that I wasn't familiar with: generations of sinning backsides had worn down the chenille around the edge, and then—this was the big difference—in the middle where the sexual urgency was dispatched too briskly by people who hadn't taken the trouble to unmake the bed. If I hadn't put it in the garbage myself years before, I really would have believed that the same one had ended up here, in a bordello. For the time being, at least, I pretended to believe it, maybe to put off the inevitable, grabbing hold of this unexpected way out as if the rest of my life depended on it: if I clung to that idea, I wouldn't have to carry out the mission I'd given myself which, now that it was attainable, had me scared.

"I asked you a question ... "

"Listen ... I'm going to ask you something that's going to sound silly, but do it and don't ask questions, I'll explain later ... "

Uneasy, perhaps because he'd sensed that I was into sado-masochism or sick sexual demands, Alan recoiled. And it was my attempt to catch him, to reassure him, that led to our first kiss. It was exchanged standing at the foot of the bed, it was long, deep, flavoured with beer and Seven-Up, and so sweet and gentle that my doubts and concerns were confused, suddenly and definitively. To hell with warnings from on high, to hell with ghostly bedspreads and ridiculous fears, I wasn't there to save my soul!

I pulled off the bedspread and sent it flying to the other end of the room, then I collapsed onto the soft mattress exhausted after years of good and loyal service.

Our lovemaking was awkward at first, but there was something exciting about our lack of experience because every move, every approach, was new and interesting and thrilling. When the hand or the mouth of the other, quickly gaining confidence, ventured into a zone we'd always thought was forbidden or unexplorable, once the surprise was over and the pleasure received or given, accepted, discreet growls or grandiose cries escaped us and peremptory and demanding on the verge of orgasm and faltering at the knowledge that we had to hold back, we asked for more, reluctantly—because we didn't want it to end, never! We weren't tired now, on the contrary, we were drunk on strength restored and desires intensified.

The odours that rose from the bed were so divine that I sometimes stopped in mid-gesture to fill my nostrils with the spicy fragrance that my North American education had always forced me to suppress. Now I was no longer holding back my penchant for everything that had to do with the sense of smell, and my feasting was complete. I'd had a foretaste of what Alan's body smelled like when we were dancing at the Tropical, but now I had him all to myself and I took advantage of it, groaning with pleasure. When I stopped for too long, Alan would ask, with his accent that drove me wild with excitement: "What's going on? Why'd you stop?" and I would answer: "Smell that! Can you see how good it smells?" My nose poked around everywhere, searching his fragrant flesh to find a new bouquet, a new aroma—and I found it, I found it every time! So did he, but more circumspectly. I, the Latin, surrendered to uncontrolled exploration; he, the more cautious Anglo-Saxon, made himself do a bit of analysis before plunging into unknown territory.

The taste matched the smell and it smelled of something I was positive I'd never be able to live without.

I lost my virginity as the sun was coming up; he lost his a few minutes later.

Bingo! Mission accomplished! Victory!

I was a consenting adult who'd consented gladly.

With the grand session over, the ceremony brought to its loud, even thundering conclusion, we both fell into a deep sleep in the bed that we'd taken by storm. Oh yes, just like animals. Like in Zola or in certain Italian films.

Just before I fell asleep, when Alan himself was going under, clinging to me as if his life depended on it, I had a comic vision of Pierrette Alarie and Richard Cassily trying to make us believe in artificial, ridiculous lovemaking in a setting of green and blue tulle curtains, and I thought that the real wedding night of Romeo and Juliet, whoever the partners were, didn't need to be set to music.

I hadn't thought of singing even once while we were making love!

*

When we woke up, we were hit by a ton of guilt. Not over loving one another as we'd done just a few hours earlier— we were rather proud of our prowess—but because we hadn't told our mothers that we weren't coming home last night. That was the sin. And that was where the danger lay.

I told Alan how beautiful I'd thought his mother was, he described how wonderful she was. Then I told him about mine, about how I adored her, how she adored me—oddly enough not one word was exchanged about our fathers— and we got to the question that preoccupied us: it was the first time either of us had stayed out all night and we were both afraid of what was waiting for us.

"I'm going to be killed." He pronounced it *touer*.

"Moi aussi, je vais me faire *touer*."

"Don't make fun of me!"

"I'm not making fun of you, I love the way you talk too much to do that ... "

"What's that, the way I talk?"

"You must know you speak French with an accent, don't you?"

"So what! Maybe you think you don't have an accent when you speak English."

"I know I do ... But isn't it sexy?"

"Sexy?"

"Yes, the way I speak English, don't you think it's sexy?"

He didn't take the time to think about it, his reply came out by itself.

"No ... I mean, I've never thought about it ... Was that what attracted you to me?"

"Not just that, but it mattered ... "

"I see ... "

"Don't give me that look, what I just said wasn't negative, Alan ... For me accents—all accents—are sexy and I think that you're particularly ... *cochon*."

"*Cochon?*"

"Yes ... More than sexy ... *dirty* you could say ... "

"You think my accent's *dirty?*"

"Do I ever!"

This time he seemed thrilled.

"And you're going to tell your mother you met an Anglo with a dirty accent?"

"Are you crazy, I could never talk to her about that! What about you?"

"Me neither ... "

"What're you going to tell to her?"

"I don't know ... Nothing. I'll make up a story she won't believe."

"Same here ... But we'll pretend we believe it and we'll have saved face."

"Face?"

"Yes ... appearances ... "

"She doesn't know?"

"She sure doesn't ... Yours?"

"God no! Will it cost you a lot, staying out last night?"

"Probably ... "

"There's always a first time ... "

"Yes."

"She'll have to get used to it ... "

"Do you think yours will be able to?"

"I don't know. No, I don't think so."

"Mine neither. We really broke all the rules, didn't we?"

"Yes."

He brought his face close to mine.

"Was I worth it at least?"

"Was I?"

To prove it to one another we made love again, our faces still marked by the vestiges of sleep and, even more, by the stiff pillows that had streaked our cheeks and scored our foreheads with hideous red lines. Both our breaths could have gagged a maggot but we didn't care. We were sticky from the night's lovemaking and that was exciting.

It lasted longer and was more gentle too, not so urgent, more refined insofar as that word could apply to our inelegant, neophyte lovemaking. Would skill come over time? I was ready to experiment as often as possible!

In the middle of our riot of caresses, when his breath was shortest and I was actually having trouble breathing because I was so busy, he took my head in his hands and asked me point-blank:

"If there was a war here between Anglos and Francos, would you be able to kill me?"

It was really not the right moment! How could anyone talk of such things in our position? In any case, the question certainly wouldn't be asked like that.

To keep from taking it seriously, I imagined myself as Scarlett O'Hara—though he was the one who was Irish!—during the Civil War, about to lose her beloved Tara. Alan was a pretty mediocre Clark Gable, I myself was light years away from Vivien Leigh, and the Saint-Louis Tourist Room bore no resemblance to a sumptuous mansion in the southern United States, but I played along and let my head fall back.

"No, Rhett, I could never do that! Do you give a damn?"

He seemed annoyed.

"I was serious."

I stuck my forehead against his and sighed.

"Of course not, I could never do that ... You know that perfectly well ... "

I thought about Arletty's lines when he came out of prison: "My heart is French but my ass is international!"—but I had a doubt. A small one. A very small one. Alan tried to lick that last doubt away, to erase it with his greedy tongue.

*

We burst into the tiny lobby of the Saint-Louis Tourist Room at a run.

"Would it be possible to use the phone? It's urgent!"

A fat slob had taken over from Jackie; I knew right away that he would be a lot less friendly than she'd been.

"With money, everything's possible."

But it was not the cashier who'd spoken, it was François Villeneuve, collapsed on the faded green plush sofa along with Carmen, who was clapping his hands as if we'd just given the performance of a lifetime.

"What are you doing here?"

"We came to wait for you ... We were going to give you another five minutes, then we were going to wake you up."

"But why are you here?"

"We're taking you out to eat at the Sélect! Everybody who scores on Saturday night goes to the Sélect at noon on Sunday to show off their trophies ... It's a tradition. Just wait, you'll laugh yourselves to death."

Alan was already dialling his number.

"I'm not a trophy ... "

"Sure you are, you're a trophy just like everybody else!"

Alan lowered his head, his voice and his tone.

"Hello? Mother? It's me ... "

François helped me into my coat. I was furious.

"How did you find out we were here? We didn't register under our real names!"

"Charly's a pal and in little hotels like this one, a crisp two-dollar bill always makes it easier to open the register ... When I saw George Sand and Donald O'Connor I got the picture ... You know, I hope, that George Sand was a woman?"

"Skip the literature lesson! What if Alan and I went home last night ... You'd have come here for nothing ... "

"You were both too ripe, the fruit had to fall! I went by my own party-boy instincts, I took a chance, and I won! Was it good at least? You can tell me, after all it was my money that made it possible for you to take the plunge!"

Carmen, who seemed to be enjoying himself tremendously, as usual, nearly disappeared behind the guitar, it was that big. François had found himself another bearer.

A heavy hand on my neck. Alan had joined us, as pale as a day in Lent.

"I have to go. Right now."

Then it was my turn to throw myself at the phone.

"Me too ... I mean, probably ... "

While I was counting the rings at the other end, François was trying to persuade Alan to stay with us. He was shaking his head without listening, like someone who's just had some disastrous news.

"Hello?" My mother's broken voice.

(Good God! The voice she reserved for grand tragedies! I don't imagine she got dressed this morning ...)

Then—a whim, independence or pure cowardice—whatever it was I merely shouted into the phone: "Mama? It's me! Don't worry, everything's fine, I'll be home late this afternoon!" Then I hung up briskly and turned towards the other three.

"I want to live this day to the full ... Let's go to the Sélect!"

But Alan was holding out a slip of paper on which he'd scrawled his phone number.

"Not me. I really can't. Give me yours if you want ... "

A knot in my heart, an unbearable weight that I would have liked to spit out before it poisoned me: I was positive I'd never see Alan again.

*

After the devastated Carré Saint-Louis—the park had once been one of the Meccas of Montreal's Francophone bourgeoisie, abandoned now to the messes left by squirrels and pigeons, its pretty fountain rusted out, its badly pruned trees now neglected—Saint-Denis Street—home for years to depressing tourist rooms that never saw a tourist and to blind pigs that were clandestine in name only and known to everybody—was even more depressing under the wet snow that had just started to fall. Wrapped in my fake camel-hair coat and not very upbeat myself, I followed François and his guitar-bearer and wondered what I was doing there, hobbling down the goddamn Sherbrooke hill for the third time in less than twelve hours, again tagging along behind this much too handsome guy who seemed to want to buy company for himself so he wouldn't be all alone.

(Did they do it on the El sofa last night? They must've ... and it can't have been a pretty sight! Why didn't they go home to do it? Or maybe they still live at home too ... Have they also got mothers who might pass out if their sons didn't come home at night? Anyway, it's not François' style, his mother must've been on his case for a long time, he must have dealt with her early on. And why am I following them like this? I don't feel like going to eat at the Sélect and to laugh at other people's trophies. Who do I think I am anyway, I haven't even got a trophy to show! My trophy left to be reviled by his mother and I'll probably never see him again. On top of everything else, I haven't even got enough money for toast and coffee! I suppose François will pay again and I'll feel obliged to do whatever he asks because I'll be indebted! And what will happen when he runs out of money, I ask you? Friendship's over, I want my ten back ... Have I just stepped onto a slippery slope that will lead me directly to ... God, how dramatic! I'm postponing the critical moment, that's all, even if I know it will be worse when I get home ... That's just it, moron, look no further: you're too big a coward to deal with a confrontation right away, so you're putting it off till later, even if you know that your mother is probably freezing the tip of her nose and the palms of her hands at the dining room window where she's been watching to see you come limping along Mont-Royal Street ... No, she doesn't know about my limp, I wasn't limping when I left the house yesterday ... But when she sees my limp it'll be even worse!)

I hadn't had enough sleep—I was used to a good eight hours and I needed it, otherwise I had trouble functioning—so there I was, staggering with fatigue, walking past the Saint-Sulpice Library and I arrived at the restaurant on my knees and nearly delirious.

The Sélect stood at the northwest corner of Saint-Denis and Sainte-Catherine. It was an immense square with fluorescent lights and rows of a greenish leather-like plastic banquettes, with service by elderly waitresses called familiarly "Mama" or "Auntie" to soften them up when they weren't in a good mood. And with the clientele they catered to, they were rarely in a good mood.

Open around the clock, at night and at early dawn the Sélect took in Montreal's most extreme partyers and the waitresses acted as bouncers as much as understanding mommies. After eating like pigs and behaving like boors, the night owls would be on their way, belching but leaving generous tips to buy forgiveness for their behaviour and their very existence. The "Mamas" and "Aunties" pocketed them, griping, as they moved on to the next table where pretty much the same thing awaited them. Afternoons, ladies who were shopping at Dupuis Frères or getting ready to attend a CKAC radio program that was broadcast from the Café Saint-Jacques, took tea as they criticized everything—the sloppy table, the questionable cleanliness of the cup, the cookie that was too dry or not dry enough, the sour milk and the waitress herself, who was really much too grouchy and ill-mannered. They sipped their tea for hours, asked for more hot water, squeezing their teabags to the last drop, then left without a tip or a thank you—after complaining to the manager who felt like strangling them too. Need I add that the staff preferred to work the night shift ...

François and Carmen filled me in on all that while we waited for a waitress to look after us, which didn't look like it would happen any time soon, because she walked right past our table without even glancing at us. François took the precaution of hiding his mouth in his fist before saying greedily:

"Something must've happened, even Auntie Juliette's in a bad mood!"

Carmen's nose was in the menu.

"Yum! I like everything here! Pancakes, eggs, spaghetti ... but what I love most of all ... "

François cut him off, shaking his head.

"Yeah, yeah, the hamburger platter, everybody knows that!"

I had indigestion, it was hard to keep my eyes open, but I asked anyway, to show I was listening and for fear that silence would fall:

"What's a hamburger platter?"

Carmen gave an apologetic and hilarious description of an ordinary hamburger—but without a bun, what a weird idea!—accompanied by fries, coleslaw and barbecue sauce. Never had a dish so simple appeared to be so complex, so divinely concocted, so beautifully presented, so delicious—and I proffered a smile that seemed to thrill the dwarf.

"All right! Finally! Have you just been at a funeral for chrissake!"

(Good God! Alan! Mama! I'd almost forgotten them for a few minutes! You're spreading yourself too thin. That's the last thing you need! This isn't where you should be!)

Auntie Juliette made a brisk and noisy entrance, as if she'd just realized we were there.

"Get a move on, order, Victor's hysterical and I'm not sure he'll make it to the end of his shift ... Since the rest of us don't feel like cooking the meal ourselves, I can't say what'll happen ... The usual, Carmen? François? You, the new boy, what do you want?"

It was too soon, I really hadn't had the time—or the appetite—to look at the menu and I stammered glumly:

"Ummm ... uhhh ... "

"Listen, I haven't got till next week, I don't know if I've even got five minutes, so make up your mind ... "

"Ummm ... uhhh ... "

"Tell me, you guys, is this a deaf-mute or is he just retarded?"

François put his hand on my menu.

"He'll have the same as me ... "

Probably thinking I was François' trophy, Auntie Juliette gave him a wink that I found insulting, then disappeared, almost at a run.

(What'm I doing here? I shouldn't be here! I should be wailing at the corner of the dining room table, asking to be forgiven and promising I'll never do it again, even though I intended to do it again the first chance I got!)

Carmen took a critical look around the restaurant. He was obviously disappointed.

"Trophies aren't what they used to be, eh François? The place isn't even full! Nobody scored last night, is that it?"

"It's too early ... By the time we're eating the place will fill up—and then the fun begins ... "

(Get up, put on your coat, get the hell out of here! They're wasting your time! And they know it! They know it and they're the ones having fun!)

"Excuse me ... I have to go to the bathroom ... "

They watched me walk away, laughing up their sleeves, or so I thought in my acute paranoia.

*

I slipped a dime into the pay phone and dialled. "Allô? Mama? It's me again. Sorry about my call a while ago ... but I'm too scared ... I'm too scared to go home ... Tell me you won't chew me out too badly, otherwise I don't know ... I don't know what to do ... I'm tired and I want to go home but I'm scared and I'm going in circles! I can't face you, Mama, what am I going to do? I'm eighteen years old and I can't face my own mother! Help!"

*

I left François and Carmen the dwarf over their steaming plates. If I'd even touched the butter-smeared eggs that sat on a bed of half-cooked bacon and turning cold while they waited, I think the grease would have poisoned me to death. To my amazement they didn't protest at all. They must have been talking about me while I was on the phone and decided to let me go, to set me free so to speak.

I promised François that I'd pay back his ten dollars as soon as I could; he pretended to believe me.

"No rush. You'll pay me back when you're rich!"

"That won't be anytime soon."

"Don't worry, nothing's going to happen anytime soon. Meanwhile—get some rest ... and say hello to your mother!"

He turned towards Carmen the dwarf who was stroking his guitar case.

Maybe I'd stopped amusing them already.

Through the door of the Sélect, which was filling up quickly, yesterday's night owls were bringing in their trophies.

Mine was the most handsome, the most interesting, certainly the nicest, and I'd let him get away. Without even asking what he did for a living.

EPILOGUE

THE ART OF THE FUGUE

Should things that are dangerous ever be said? Or should we keep them to ourselves? That was the dilemma in which I found myself on that snowy, grey January afternoon while my friends, who'd left a message for me, were sitting peacefully in some movie theatre, laughing at Jerry Lewis's latest antics or blowing their noses at Susan Hayward's latest woes.

Meanwhile, Mama was glued to her rocking chair in the corner of the dining room—had she even left it since I went out the night before, just after supper?—and danger floated in the air between us, the danger that she would *find out*, the danger that she would *condemn*.

Candide was home from his journey around the world only to learn that it was better to cultivate one's garden; Pinocchio, regurgitated by the whale, had become a real little boy because he'd sworn to obey Geppetto, his creator and now his father; Hansel and Gretel, with the wicked witch roasted medium rare and the gingerbread children returned to their normal state, had promised never again to stray away from home—or so I'd retained from those three stories, two of which had lulled my childhood and the third, because of its euphoric absurdity and its virulent social content, had delighted my adolescence. I too was coming home from my peregrinations, but if I was ashamed of anything, it was of my own cowardice—not of what I had done. No, of that I was quite proud and I had no intention of giving it up: I would not cultivate my garden, I would not swear obedience to my progenitors, and it was out of the question that I promise not to stray from home. The threshold had been crossed, the taste of freedom was still on my lips, and we weren't living in a moral tale.

There too was a dilemma: whether to lie outright, make up a story (a fairy tale, in fact) which my mother wouldn't believe at all but to which she too could cling to avoid looking further, or to tell the truth (François, Carmen, Alan, pandemonium, the Saint-Louis Tourist Room—blunt reality!), confess my goals, my deeds, my pride and risk the wrath of heaven and—who knows—maybe even banishment.

As the hopeless asshole that I was, I obviously opted for a clever mixture of the two, which wasn't all that obvious, as it happens: I invented a party with some friends from the Institut des Arts Graphiques I'd run into at the opera (far-fetched, but if told with sincerity it could pass), confessed to consuming various alcoholic beverages (among Québécois at that time, booze was much less serious than sex) and the situation in which I found myself when I realized that it was two a.m., that I was in ... in ... Saint-Léonard de Port-Maurice and that I couldn't go home or call because it was so late, that's it, and my fear of how she would react when I woke up this morning. I secretly hoped that she'd trap me, hound me, that she'd see all the gaping holes in my story, that she'd find me out and astonish me. I didn't want to confess, I was absolutely incapable of it—I wanted to be exposed!

But her own mask was so impenetrable that I didn't know where I stood. If she guessed everything and was managing to hide it from me, out of prudishness or shame, I'd never know, nor would I know what purpose was served by that double masquerade, the mutual lie, the deliberately indirect questions and the perfectly invented responses.

(Why talk to each other if you don't intend to say anything? But it's up to you, idiot, go on, give her a *shocking* answer, provoke her—maybe that's what she wants!)

When I gesticulated, I could smell Alan on my hands and I hoped that she'd pick it up (smell me, Mama, I smell of sex! At last, I smell of sex, be happy for me!), hoped that she'd frown, that she'd bend over me and tell me—just so I'd understand that she understood—to go and get washed. As for me, I had the crazy idea to never wash again! Never! I went so far as to lay my hand on her arm so that Alan would be attached to her skin. But if she smelled anything she didn't let me know, and the perils with which I'd peppered my answers to her urgent questions were eventually lost in the trivial tag-ends of our conversation.

"Don't you ever do that to me again."

"I'm not going to wake you up in the small hours of the morning, you'd kill me!"

(My God, Alan, are you doing the same thing as me—lying shamefully to avoid explanations that would be too complicated and too hard to make?)

"I'll tell you one thing: there isn't going to be a next time."

"Mama, I'm eighteen years old, nineteen in five months, don't ask me for too much! There'll be other parties! Maybe even more and more of them ... "

(That's good, prepare her!)

"Just tell me in advance ... "

"Those parties don't get planned in advance, Mama (liar!). I mean the parties do, but not what's going to happen at them ... "

"Exactly, let's talk about that, about what happened ... I'm warning you, as far as staying out all night's concerned, little boy, forget it as long as you're living under my roof! As long as you live here you're going to come home and sleep in your own bed, in your pyjamas, understand? Eighteen or not eighteen! Where did you spend the night anyway? On the floor, like a drunk?"

"What's that? Ummm ... on a sofa ... "

"A sofa that opens up?"

"No, just a sofa ... An ordinary sofa."

"By yourself?"

"Mama, if I wasn't by myself do you think I'd tell you?"

(Say something! React!)

"There was just room for one on the sofa."

"What about the others, where did they sleep?"

"What others?"

"The other guests ... You weren't all by yourself in the middle of Saint-Léonard de Port-Maurice ... Where did the rest of them sleep?"

"Some of them had cars ... "

"Which means you could've had a lift?"

"There were just two ... just two people had cars and they were full ... Anyway, I felt like sleeping there! It reminded me of the pyjama parties when I was a child ... "

"Except that you didn't have pyjamas ... "

"I didn't sleep naked, Mama, if it makes you feel any better. I slept in my clothes."

"And the mother let you?"

"Mama, I just told you, the guy's got an apartment in Saint-Léonard, his parents live in Granby!"

"They must be rich."

"I don't know ... maybe ... "

"And he doesn't go home to Granby for the weekend? And his parents let him give parties? Did they know that their child was giving that party?"

"He's not a child, he's twenty years old!"

"You should be with people your own age!"

"We talked about that too, Mama. We're going around in circles! What the heck are you doing, are you testing me to see if I'm lying?"

(Yes, please, go on, insist! At least ask me if there were just guys—though maybe you'd be even more worried if there'd been girls ...)

"I'm asking you questions because I want some answers!"

(Do you really? Are you sure you want to hear the answers?)

"I could make some up."

A stern look, like the ones she gave me as a child when I'd seriously misbehaved.

"I'd know."

"So why are you pushing it? You must know I'm not lying!"

(Asshole! Coward! You're telling lies to her face and maybe she knows!)

"Meanwhile, go and get washed ... "

(Huh? What?)

"You reek of alcohol."

(I can't believe it, Mama, I can't believe it! It's not true! I wasn't drinking! I had one sip of beer and that was more than twelve hours ago! Don't believe me, I beg you, don't believe me! Go on, go on, you're burning up!)

"Your brother ... "

(Oh no, not him ...)

"My brother's my brother and I'm me."

"Don't interrupt, you know I can't stand that! Your brother is thirty years old and he's never stayed out all night even once!"

"That doesn't mean anything! Maybe it just means that he does in the daytime what you think I did last night!

Maybe he lives his bachelor life in the daytime, but I don't!"

(That's the last perch I'm offering you, grab hold of it, I beg you, grab hold of it!)

"How can you say such a thing about your own older brother, he's a gentleman, he's so sensible he's practically a monk ... "

The Sermon on the Mount was underway, our conversation was over, and it was my fault, I was the one who'd steered her in this direction. I knew it though, I knew that when my mother talked about my brother she'd get carried away, lose all objectivity, all sense of proportion, and the only thing to do was let her rave and hope she wouldn't change the subject. But I knew she talked about me the same way when I wasn't there ...

I listened to her sing my older brother's praises, thinking I'd rather she despised me or even disowned me.

(I know he's perfect and I'm not, so why don't you pay some attention to me! Find out that I'm even less perfect than you think—and react!)

But maybe it was one last trick on her part; maybe she wanted to provoke me by talking about my brother's supposed perfection to make *me* react, make me let the cat out of the bag, no matter what kind it was, no matter what nasty surprise he had in his jaws.

She adored me as much as my brother, I knew that, but I was afraid that this character flaw of mine—or at least what she considered to be a flaw when it was actually my most important trait, I was now convinced—the damage I could inflict on her love for me, the knowledge that I was a man but a man different from others, would kill her. Or me. Or annihilate both of us in an inferno of incomprehension, injustice, and irreparable misunderstanding.

I stared at her to make her understand, she looked away and fiddled with the hem of her flowered dress.

And I retreated and ran myself a bath.

*

A timid knock on the bathroom door, barely perceptible, as if it really didn't want to be heard.

"Now what is it? Can't I take a bath in peace?"

I knew that what was going to come would be important, Mama never disturbed me during my ablutions, but I chose to be aggressive so that she couldn't sense my concern through the wall.

"I only wanted to tell you ... "

I pictured her with her forehead on the door, in the role of She Who Confesses while I was the one who had sinned.

" ... I just wanted to tell you I don't want you thinking I'm an idiot ... I'm old enough, I've lived, I've seen how others live, figured out what they're like ... "

I sat up in the water to hear the rest, to sense absolution coming, to catch it on the wing and immerse myself in once and for all.

" ... Actually, what I wanted to tell you is that you'll still be my child."

(Thank you, Mama! Thank you, Mama! But I'm sorry, I can't let it out!)

"Do you understand?"

(Say it! Say it! Just one little sound! You can make one little sound! She's the one asking you if you understand!)

"Yes."

*

I had placed next to the record player the opera albums that had my favourite love duets. The inevitable *Faust* and *Carmen* of course, but also *Tristan und Isolde* and its brilliant second act, the longest, wildest love duet of all time; *Un Ballo in Maschera*—two lovers beneath a gallows, what an image! *Madama Butterfly*, for its scent of cherry blossoms and its hokey and oh so touching Japanese artifacts; and above all, *Otello*, Verdi's version, whose first act ends with the Moor and Desdemona crushed by the crystalline sounds of the vault of heaven—"*Un baccio, un altro baccio* ... " But to make me cry because I needed to badly, I'd set aside *La Bohème* and its overwhelming third act.

I was stretched out on the living room sofa, my ear practically glued to the speaker, and I'd closed my eyes.

(Where are you right now, Alan? Are you crying, like me? Were you punished, did you simply skate the way I did, are you, like me, both relieved and ashamed, have you got my phone number in the little pocket of your shirt, is it pressed against your heart? But anyway, thank you!)

Although I stuffed my fingers in my nose as deep as I could, the goddamn soap had erased all traces of Alan and it was as if nothing had happened. As for my marrowbone, it smelled of stale smoke and tepid beer.

That's it, here it comes ...

"Mimì è tanto malata!"